Invasion of the Body Squeezers

Part II

Look for more books in the Goosebumps Series 2000
by R.L. Stine:

#1 Cry of the Cat
#2 Bride of the Living Dummy
#3 Creature Teacher
#4 Invasion of the Body Squeezers, Part I

Invasion of the Body Squeezers

Part II

AN
APPLE
PAPERBACK

SCHOLASTIC INC.
New York Toronto London Auckland Sydney

A PARACHUTE PRESS BOOK

ISBN 0-590-39992-6

Copyright © 1998 by Parachute Press, Inc.
All rights reserved. Published by Scholastic Inc.
APPLE PAPERBACKS and logo are trademarks and/or registered trademarks of Scholastic Inc.
GOOSEBUMPS is a registered trademark
of Parachute Press, Inc.

12 11 10 9 8 7 6 5 4 3 2 1   8 9/9 0 1 2 3/0

Printed in the U.S.A.   40

First Scholastic printing, May 1998

The Story So Far . . .

My name is Jack Archer, and I live in Los Angeles.

An alien creature has invaded Earth. It's in my bedroom right now. And I don't think it's friendly!

But do you think anyone will believe me?

No. My friends tease me and call me Saucerman because I've spotted some UFOs, aliens, and weird creatures — that didn't exactly turn out to be UFOs, aliens, and weird creatures.

Okay, okay. I made a few mistakes. But why won't anyone believe me now?

Part of the problem is my little sister, Billie. She is always trying to compete with me, always trying to top me. If I say I saw a flying saucer, Billie immediately claims she saw *two* flying saucers — and they were bigger than mine!

1

Last summer, I spent a lot of time spying on my neighbor Mr. Fleshman. I was convinced that Mr. Fleshman was hiding some kind of strange creature in his house.

One night, Mr. Fleshman appeared at my front door. He acted very scary. He warned me to stop spying on him. He told me his work was top secret. That made me even more eager to find out the truth about Mr. Fleshman.

At the end of summer, a strange meteor appeared over the earth. Scientists were puzzled by it. I spent hours in my backyard trying to see it.

One afternoon, while I was searching for the meteor, I spotted a creature in Mr. Fleshman's window. Mr. Fleshman didn't seem to be home. I sneaked inside. I found a photo album, filled with photos of strange green creatures. And I found a coffin in an empty room. It started to open.

I admit I was *creeped out*! I ran into the hall — and a terrifying ghost formed out of mist and swept over me.

Mr. Fleshman popped out. He laughed at my fright. He explained to me that he works in the movies. He designs monsters and special effects. That's why his work is top secret.

How did I feel? Very relieved.

But here's where things turned *terrifying*!

I accidentally took a small electronic box from Mr. Fleshman's house. Back in my room, I began to hear voices from the box. The voices controlled me. They made me act really strange.

I know my teachers and parents were worried about me. They thought the news stories about the meteor in the sky frightened me.

But I kept listening to the voices in the little box. I realized the voices were alien creatures speaking from outer space — and they were preparing to land on Earth.

Why did Mr. Fleshman have this box? I tried to return it to him — and I overheard Mr. Fleshman on the phone. "We are ready for them," Mr. Fleshman was saying. "We will defeat them. They will not stand a chance."

Wow. What a shock. Mr. Fleshman lied to me. He wasn't a movie special-effects designer. He was a government agent who planned to battle the invading aliens.

Soon after that amazing discovery, I had another one. I saw a flash of light in the sky. A meteorite fell to Earth. It landed at my feet!

I was thrilled. So excited, I could barely speak! I picked it up and carried it into the house.

My parents didn't believe I'd found a meteorite. Billie didn't help matters. She claimed to find a meteorite of her own!

I was *desperate* for someone to believe me. I took the space object to school to show to Mr. Liss, my science teacher.

But my two friends, Henry Glover and Derek Lee, thought that Saucerman was making up wild stories again. They picked up the meteorite and begin to toss it back and forth like a ball.

I was so furious! Why won't anyone ever take me seriously? I grabbed the space object and ran out of school. I ran home and put it on my dresser.

Whoa! To my shock, it began to rumble. It cracked open. A small, insectlike creature climbed out. I stared in amazement, watching the creature grow . . . and grow.

It grew into an ugly, frightening monster.

It lowered itself to the floor. And then it staggered across the room, arms outstretched, ready to attack . . .

froze in horror. I couldn't breathe. My mouth dropped open, but I couldn't make a sound.

The space alien stared across my bedroom at me. I could see my reflection in its oval black eyes.

Behind it on the dresser, the small, round meteorite glowed, washing the room in an eerie green.

I swallowed hard, my mouth as dry as sandpaper. My heart pounded so hard, my chest hurt.

The alien had climbed out from the space object, tiny as a grasshopper. As it stretched and stepped onto the dresser top, it began to grow.

Bigger. Bigger than an insect. The slender body thickened. The green head inflated.

As big as a lizard, it climbed down the front of the dresser. Walking headfirst on all fours. Leaving a thick trail of milky slime behind it.

The creature lowered itself to the floor and stood on its hind legs. Slender green arms twined out from its body. It stretched and grew taller than the dresser.

Taller than me!

Its oval black eyes grew. The shiny green head inflated like a balloon. I saw two deep nostrils and a small, lipless mouth.

Hands formed on the slender arms. They curled into fists, then opened, four tubelike fingers on each hand.

The alien stared at me without blinking, without any expression at all on its face. As it grew, its body shimmered wetly.

It opened its mouth, revealing two curled tusks and rows of pointed teeth. A cap of green skin formed over its forehead, curved and hard like a turtle shell.

It stepped unsteadily away from the dresser. I saw puddles of milky slime on the floor behind it.

SQUISH.

Its feet spread out on the floor, making a wet smacking sound with each step.

It spread its arms. Raised them out at its sides. And took another heavy, wet step toward me.

I finally forced my trembling legs to move. I stumbled back.

My legs hit the bed.

I toppled over. Landed in a sitting position on the bedspread.

"Are — are you *friendly*?" I choked out in a tiny voice.

It didn't reply.

Stretching out its arms, the alien took another heavy step toward me.

"My name is Jack!" I cried. "Do you have a name?"

I squinted at the throbbing, growing creature through the pulsing green glow.

Please be friendly! I prayed silently. *Please be friendly!*

"Do you have a name? *Do* you?" My voice came out so high and shrill.

I jumped shakily to my feet. "Jack," I repeated, slapping myself on the chest. "Jack."

No reply.

"Welcome to Earth," I choked out. "Do you know you've landed on Earth?"

The creature's eyes widened, no longer dark ovals. Now they glowed, round and red. Staring hard at me, it lowered its head. Hunched its shoulders.

Preparing to attack?

I glanced quickly at my bedroom door. It seemed a million miles away. Could I get over there? Could I escape before the creature made a grab for me?

"Can you speak?" I cried. "Do you have a name? Are you friendly?"

The alien opened its mouth wide and let out a

7

breathy hiss. It sounded like air escaping from a balloon. Two rows of curved tusks slid out from the open mouth.

It clicked its teeth together. Clicked them once, twice.

It's going to eat me! I decided.

It stared at me hungrily, clicking its teeth.

I knew I had to move. If I stood there one more second, I'd be lunch.

I took a deep breath. I tensed my leg muscles.

The alien reached out both arms for me.

Move! I ordered myself.

A fierce cry burst from my throat. I lowered my head and lurched to the door.

Another long hiss escaped the creature's open mouth. I saw it swing around. Its eyes bulged and rolled. It turned heavily and lumbered after me.

"No! Please!" I didn't even realize I was screaming, pleading with it. "Please —!"

I reached the door, my chest heaving.

SQUISH.

The alien took another heavy, wet step.

I forced myself through the door. Into the hall.

"Help me!" I shrieked. "Somebody —!"

But of course no one else was home. It was the middle of the afternoon. My little sister, Billie, was still at school. Mom and Dad were at work.

No one there.

No one to help.

No one to see this *thing*, this alien creature.

This *hungry* alien creature.

Hissing with each step, it lumbered into the hall. Its head bounced low over hunched shoulders as it moved steadily toward me.

"Oh, help! Oh, please!"

I was too terrified *not* to scream.

I dove for the stairs. Nearly fell. Grabbed the banister to stop myself.

Then I hurtled down, two at a time, the heavy thud of my sneakers echoing through the empty house.

I reached the bottom, breathing hard.

Whirled around. And saw the creature at the top of the stairs.

"No — please! Help me, somebody!"

It stretched out its arms — thick arms now, no longer slender, now so thick and muscular. It stretched out its arms as if reaching for me and trodded down the stairs.

I backed away from it. Backed to the front door. Tugged the door open without turning around.

"No! Please!" I stared up at the creature, halfway down the stairs. Stared at the bulging eyes, the open, hissing mouth, the curled, clicking tusks and pointed teeth.

The four-fingered hands, grasping for me, reaching, reaching.

"No —!" I uttered another terrified cry.

I bumped open the screen door.

Stepped back. Stepped back. My eyes still on the creature lumbering down the stairs.

Stepped back. Onto the front lawn.

And bumped hard into *another creature*.

"Nooooo!" A horrified wail escaped my throat as it wrapped its arms around me from behind.

2

With a sharp cry, I shoved the hands away and stumbled free.

I spun around — and cried out in surprise. "Mr. Liss!"

Breathing hard, my science teacher squinted through his glasses into the bright sunlight at me. Sweat rolled down his forehead. His normally slicked-down hair was wild and blown back. He looked as if he'd run all the way from school.

"Jack, are you okay?" he demanded breathlessly.

"No —" I choked out. "No. I —"

"I didn't mean to scare you," he said, tucking the bottom of his long-sleeved blue pullover shirt into his gray slacks. He is tall and lanky and always tugging and fiddling with his clothing. "You ran out of class, and I was worried about you."

"It — it's *in* there!" I stammered. I pointed frantically to the open front door.

"Excuse me?" Mr. Liss wiped the sweat from his forehead with the back of his hand. "I don't understand, Jack. I saw you were upset, so I hurried over here. But —"

"In there!" I cried. "A space creature. It's in my house!"

I knew I wasn't making any sense. I couldn't help it. I couldn't think clearly. My panic had totally frozen my brain. I could hardly form words!

I startled him by grabbing his hand. It felt hot and wet. I pointed to the door. "See it? Do you see it?"

We both stared at the open door.

Nothing there.

Over my panting breaths, I listened for the creature's repeated hisses.

Silence.

An airplane floated high overhead. I could hear the distant drone of its engines. Somewhere down the block a baby cried.

"I don't see anything, Jack," Mr. Liss said softly, still fussing with the front of his shirt.

"It's in there!" I cried. "It's in my house. You've *got* to believe me!"

"Okay, okay," he said, nearly in a whisper. He made calming motions with both hands. "Take a deep breath, Jack. Count to twenty."

"No —!" I wailed. "You don't understand!" I kept my eyes on the door, expecting the ugly space creature to burst out, clicking its teeth, stretching out its powerful arms to grab me.

"It's *in* there, Mr. Liss!" I insisted, my voice cracking. "I was right. That wasn't a meteorite. It was some kind of spacecraft. Everyone laughed at me. But the creature was inside it. And now —"

"Let's go see," Mr. Liss replied softly. He started toward the house.

"Huh?" I gasped.

He narrowed his eyes at me. "Let's check it out."

"No — wait!" I cried.

But he moved quickly, taking two long strides onto the front steps. I held back, hands pressed against my face as he pulled open the screen door.

I held my breath, waiting for his shocked scream.

He turned back to me, his eyeglasses filling with sunlight. "I don't see anything, Jack." He smoothed his windblown hair. "All quiet."

He started into the house, motioning for me to follow.

I hesitated. "Be careful," I said. "It's in there. It's really big, Mr. Liss. Bigger than a human, and —"

The screen door slammed as Mr. Liss disappeared into the house.

My heart started to pound as I made my way onto the front steps. I peered into the house through the screen door.

"Mr. Liss?" I called in.

No reply.

I shielded my eyes with my hands. Where was he? How had he disappeared so quickly?

"Mr. Liss?" I called in, a little louder.

A cold chill shook my entire body. Had something terrible happened to him already?

Did the creature attack him as soon as he entered the house?

Attack him so quickly, so silently?

I grabbed the screen door handle and pulled it open.

Taking a deep breath, I poked my head in.

"Mr. Liss? Mr. Liss?"

I stepped shakily into the front hall. The screen door hit my back as it closed. I jumped forward.

And listened.

Silence.

Then I heard scraping footsteps approaching from the back of the house.

The creature!

I gasped. Prepared to run back outside.

No. Wait. The footsteps were too light. Too fast.

Mr. Liss appeared, walking rapidly, hands in his pockets. "Nothing in the kitchen," he reported. He eyed me for a long moment. "Should we check the downstairs bedrooms?"

I swallowed hard. "No!" I choked out. "Let's just go! Let's get *out* of here! We have to get help!"

He studied me for a long moment. "Maybe you had a bad nightmare, Jack. Sometimes when a person is upset, his imagination can play tricks on him."

"No!" I protested. "It's real. You've got to believe me."

"Then let's see if we can find it," he insisted. He turned and started down the hall.

I hurried after him. I didn't want to be alone. I didn't want to face the creature alone.

I followed Mr. Liss into my parents' bedroom. The white curtains fluttered in front of the open window. A long rectangle of sunlight slanted across the bed.

No sign of the alien creature.

"It's big and it's dangerous," I said in a whisper. "We have to get out of here, Mr. Liss. We have to —"

Frowning, he loped across the hall to the guest bedroom. He poked his head inside, then quickly turned back to me.

"I don't see anything, Jack. And I don't hear anything strange."

"But — but —" I sputtered.

He pulled off his glasses and wiped the lenses with the sleeve of his shirt. As he cleaned them, he squinted hard at me.

"I know you were really upset at school," he said. "I know you were unhappy about the kids tossing your ball around."

16

"It wasn't a ball!" I cried shrilly. "It was a space-craft. It landed in my yard, Mr. Liss. And the creature came out of it."

The science teacher pulled the glasses back on and continued to squint at me. "You shouldn't have run away from school —" he started.

But I didn't let him finish. I shook my fists in the air and shrieked at him. *"I'm telling the truth! There's a space creature in this house — and it's going to eat us both!"*

Mr. Liss's mouth opened in surprise at my outburst. "Jack —"

I didn't give him a chance to say anything. I took off down the hall, running to the front door. "We have to get the police," I cried. "We have to get help. It's too big. It's too dangerous!"

I ran into the front hall — and stopped short. A shocked cry escaped my throat.

I gaped at the creature, its head hunched over its glistening green shoulders, mouth open, revealing its curled teeth, powerful arms outstretched.

I gaped at the creature, blocking the front door.

Blocking my escape.

"**O**h, my," I heard Mr. Liss murmur. "Oh, my. Oh, my."

"See?" I whispered.

Mr. Liss nodded, his mouth open, his eyes bulging. "Oh, my." He swept both hands back through his brown hair.

I swallowed hard. "It's blocking the door," I managed to say in a tiny voice.

"I'm sorry," Mr. Liss whispered. "Sorry I didn't believe you."

The creature hissed and clicked its teeth. Its big eyes rolled around in its head. Its whole body heaved wetly as it took a step away from the door.

"We've got to get away," I said, tugging at the teacher's sleeve. "We've got to get help."

Mr. Liss didn't take his eyes from the alien. "We've got to get a camera!" he declared.

The creature took another heavy step toward us. It stretched its arms out wide, rolling its tube-like fingers. It opened and shut its jaws, its long tusks scraping noisily.

"Mr. Liss, come on!" I insisted. I pulled his arm, trying to tug him toward the back of the house.

But he pulled free of me. "We're going to be famous, Jack," he said breathlessly. "We are the first people on Earth ever to see a being from another planet."

"But if it eats us . . ." I started.

The creature lumbered forward. Its whole body pulsed and bounced as it moved toward us.

"Mr. Liss, please!" I begged.

But the teacher ignored me. He took a step toward the creature. "We are Earthlings!" he shouted to it. "Can you speak? Where are you from?"

The alien stretched out its arms. It opened its mouth in a wet hiss.

"I already tried talking to it!" I declared. "It didn't answer."

I took a step back as the creature moved into the hallway. Closer. Closer.

"Please! We've got to get out!" I shrieked.

Mr. Liss finally turned to me. "I think it's friendly," he said, his voice cracking with excitement.

"Huh?" I gasped.

"I do." The teacher nodded. "I think it's friendly.

Look, Jack. It has its arms outstretched. I think it wants a hug."

I took another step back. My heart pounded so hard, I could barely breathe.

"No," I insisted. "It's a trick, Mr. Liss."

"I really think it wants a hug," the teacher replied.

"No! Stay away!" I cried. "It's so ugly! It's so evil!"

Mr. Liss shook his head. "It can't help looking different from us. It's an alien from another planet. But that doesn't mean it's evil."

He took another step toward the pulsing, hissing creature. "I think the alien is trying to greet us, Jack. I think it wants to hug us."

"Mr. Liss — no!" I begged. "Let's go! Please!"

But the teacher ignored my cries.

He stepped forward to greet the alien.

The alien stretched out both its arms. Mr. Liss stretched out both his arms.

And they hugged.

"Oh, my," Mr. Liss murmured.

The creature's green arms wrapped gently around the teacher's shoulders.

"Oh, my," the teacher repeated. "Do you see, Jack? I was right."

Mr. Liss didn't turn around. The creature hugged him tighter. Then it lowered its big green head and pressed it against Mr. Liss's cheek.

"It's a warm-blooded creature, like us," the science teacher reported. "Do you see, Jack? It's friendly. I knew it. I —"

Mr. Liss stopped talking with a gasp.

I saw the creature tighten its arms around him.

"Hey," the teacher groaned. "Wait. Stop —"

The creature's huge head pressed against Mr. Liss's face.

The muscular arms spread around the teacher's slender body.

Tighter.

Mr. Liss groaned again. Then, as I stood behind him watching helplessly, Mr. Liss started to struggle. "Hey, let go! Let go!"

5

"Mr. Liss!" I cried.

I watched in horror as the creature's powerful arms tightened around the teacher's waist.

Mr. Liss groaned in pain. He struggled and squirmed, trying to wrestle free. His glasses flew off and clattered across the floor. His eyes bulged. His face twisted in terror.

The creature pressed its head against Mr. Liss's cheek and let out short, hissing breaths. *HISS . . . HISS . . . HISS . . .*

"Can't . . . breathe . . ." Mr. Liss gasped.

I searched frantically around the hallway for a weapon. Something to throw at the creature. Something to hit it with.

I spotted a tall, glass flower vase on a table outside the living room. I dove for it. Grabbed it in both hands.

I raised it high, preparing to send it crashing down on the creature.

"Noooo!" I let out a scream when I saw the creature's big hands go up. Its tubelike fingers spread. And long silvery nails shot out from the fingers.

The gleaming nails slid out until they were at least a foot long! And then the creature pushed them into Mr. Liss's back.

Mr. Liss uttered a cry. His eyes bulged in horror.

The vase fell from my hands and dropped to the floor with a heavy *THUD*.

I started to choke.

I'm not seeing this! I told myself.

This isn't happening!

The long nails slid straight through the teacher's shirt. Into his back. Slid inside Mr. Liss, as if he were made of air.

I watched its big hands totally slide inside Mr. Liss's back. Then its arms.

The alien lowered a shoulder, hunched its head. The shoulder pushed into the teacher's back. The green head made a wet, slapping sound as it slid inside.

"No! No! No! Oh, no!" Mr. Liss chanted, mouth open wide in fright. His arms shot up in the air. His eyes rolled frantically in his head.

"No! No! No!"

The creature's knees bent. It tilted forward. And then *leaped* off the floor.

Leaped into Mr. Liss's back.

And vanished.

Vanished inside the teacher.

"No! No! No!" Mr. Liss continued to chant. His arms flew wildly above his head.

I staggered back against the wall. My chest heaved. I struggled to breathe. I covered my ears to block out the teacher's horrified chant.

"No! No! No!"

And I stared at Mr. Liss's back.

At his shirt. Smooth now. Not a wrinkle. Not a hole or a tear.

No bulge. No wound. No blood.

The shirt had come untucked in the struggle. It was stained with sweat under the arms. But I could see no sign of the creature.

It had vanished. Pushed itself inside Mr. Liss.

The teacher's cries stopped suddenly. Breathing hard, he lowered his arms. He scrambled to tuck in his shirt.

"Mr. Liss?" I finally managed to call out his name.

He squinted at me, as if not recognizing me. Then he bent and picked up his glasses.

"Mr. Liss? Are you okay?" I choked out, my back still pressed hard against the wall. My legs so trembly and weak.

He slid the glasses onto his face. Then he brushed back his hair with one hand. He shook his head as if trying to clear it.

Then he started to hum. Softly. Just musical notes. Not a tune. He hummed to himself, staring blankly at me.

"Mr. Liss?" I whispered. "It's me. Jack. Are you okay?"

He continued to hum. Then he smacked his lips together. Smacked them several times, making kissing sounds.

He scratched his right shoulder. Then he scratched the back of his neck. Scratching hard, so hard that the skin reddened.

I've got to get out of here, I decided.

Mr. Liss isn't right. The creature pushed inside him. And now Mr. Liss isn't right.

He started humming again. Just notes, crazy notes. Not a song. As he hummed, he scratched his neck, then his shoulder.

"Uh . . . I'll go get help," I said. I started to slide along the wall toward the front door.

Mr. Liss stopped humming. He lowered his hand and moved to block my path.

He clicked his tongue. "T-t-t. I'm okay, Jack," he said. He spoke so slowly, one word at a time.

"No. I'll get someone," I insisted. "You wait here, Mr. Liss. I'll be back as soon as I find someone to help."

"No. Really," the teacher insisted. A strange

25

half-smile formed on his lips. "I'm perfectly t-t okay."

And as he smiled at me, something green bulged out of both of his ears. It looked like bubblegum bubbles, inflating. Like green balloons growing out of his ears.

"I — I'll get a doctor or someone," I stammered, inching toward the open door.

"T-t-t. I don't need a doctor," he replied, still smiling. "I've never felt better, Jack." The green bubbles bobbed on both sides of his face. Then they silently deflated and slid back into his ears.

"It's *inside* you!" I screamed. The words burst from my mouth. I had controlled my panic for so long. But I couldn't hold it in any longer.

"The alien disappeared! It went *inside* you, Mr. Liss. I saw it!"

He shook his head. "No. I'm t-t-t fine." He took a step toward me, that strange half-smile frozen on his face. Behind his glasses, his eyes stared straight ahead at me. They didn't move. They didn't blink.

The green bubbles poked out of his ears again. Bobbed for a few seconds. Then disappeared back into his head.

"I'm going for help!" I cried.

But he blocked my way.

"Don't t-t be afraid, Jack," he said softly.

"I *am* afraid!" I shrieked. "It's inside you, Mr. Liss. Don't you understand? I've got to get help!"

He shook his head again. Then he spread out his arms. His eyes burned into mine. "Give me a hug, Jack," he whispered.

"Huh?" I gasped and stepped back.

"Give me a t-t hug," the teacher repeated, stretching out his arms. "It wants to spread itself to you too. Then it will be inside both of us."

"No —" I gasped.

"It wants to t-t-t spread out, to spread itself to everyone," Mr. Liss continued. "Won't that be *wonderful*?"

He stepped toward me, his shoes scraping heavily over the floor. Green bubbles poked from his ears, then slid back in.

I took another step back. Then another.

"Just a quick hug," Mr. Liss insisted. He clicked several times. "A quick hug, Jack. We have to spread out. We have to hug everyone. It's okay. Really. T-t. I'm perfectly okay."

My back hit the wall. "No — please!" I cried. "I don't want to. You're *not* okay! You're *weird*! You're *possessed*!"

"No," he replied softly, shuffling closer. His shoes scraped along the floor, as if they were too heavy for him to lift.

"A quick hug, Jack," he insisted. "Be one of the first. You're so lucky to be one of the first."

"Noooo!" I wailed.

I pushed myself off the wall and sprang past him, into the living room. And cried out when I saw Mom and Billie enter from the back. "You're home!"

Mom dropped her briefcase on the table and turned to me. "Jack? What's going on? Why are you home so early?"

I spun around and pointed at Mr. Liss with a trembling hand. "He's got the *creature* inside him!" I shrieked. "Stop him! Stop him! It's *inside* him!"

Mom's mouth dropped open. She stared wide-eyed at Mr. Liss.

The teacher hadn't moved from the front hallway. His arms were still outstretched, still ready to hug.

"A creature landed! From outer space!" I told Mom. "It — it went *into* him!" I cried.

Billie stared across the room at Mr. Liss. "I have a creature from outer space inside me too!" she declared. She stuck out her arms and began to stagger around the room. "I'm an alien! I'm an alien!"

"Billie — shut up!" I screamed.

Mr. Liss tossed back his head and laughed. "Both of your kids have wonderful t-t imaginations, Mrs. Archer." He moved into the living room, straightening his shirt and taking those heavy, shuffling steps.

"Yes, they certainly do," Mom agreed quickly. She flashed me a bewildered look.

Billie was walking stiff-legged like a robot now. "I *am* a creature from outer space!" she declared. She started to cough.

"Billie — upstairs," Mom ordered. "She has a bad sore throat. I brought her home from school early. I think her tonsils are acting up again." She walked up to Mr. Liss.

"Mom — stay away from him!" I cried desperately. "He's possessed by the alien! You've got to listen to me!"

Mr. Liss chuckled. He stuck out a hand to shake hands with Mom. "I'm Ted Liss," he said. "I'm t-t-t Jack's science teacher."

"Nice to meet you, Mr. Liss," Mom said. She raised her hand to shake his.

"No —!" I screamed and pulled her hand away.

"Jack!" Mom cried sharply. "What is your problem?"

"Don't touch him!" I wailed. "I'm telling the truth, Mom! The alien! It hugged him and then —"

"Stop it right now," Mom demanded, gritting her teeth. She pressed a hand over my mouth. "I mean it, Jack. Silence. Not another word."

She slowly lowered her hand from my mouth and turned to Mr. Liss. "I'm sorry. Jack has been

30

very upset about all the news stories about the meteor."

Mr. Liss nodded solemnly. "Yes. I t-t understand."

"But — but —" I sputtered.

Mom raised her hand. "Not another word!" she shouted.

I bit my lip. Why wouldn't she listen to me? We were all in terrible danger. And she didn't care. She only cared about being polite to my teacher.

Mom turned back to him. "I apologize for Jack's outbursts. His father and I are really very worried about him."

"Well . . . there was a problem in school today," Mr. Liss said, scratching his shoulder.

Mom's mouth fell open again. "A problem?"

Mr. Liss nodded. He clicked his tongue three times. "That's why I'm here. Some of the students were teasing Jack. He ran out of the school. I followed him home to make sure he was okay."

Mom frowned at me. She placed a hand gently on my shoulder. "Jack — you're trembling!" she exclaimed. "Are you feeling okay? Maybe you should go up to your room and lie down."

"I'm not sick!" I demanded. "You've got to listen to me, Mom. That meteorite — it was really a spacecraft. An alien climbed out and —"

Mom squeezed my shoulder. "Sshhh. Try to calm down. It'll be okay."

"I'd better be going," Mr. Liss said to my mom. He began to shuffle heavily out of the room. "I'm sorry if I startled you. I wanted to make sure Jack was okay."

"That was very nice of you, Mr. Liss." Mom followed him to the door.

"Mom, please —" I pleaded. "Don't let him touch you!"

"Jack!" Mom cried. "I really think you need to go lie down. I'm going to call Dr. Bendix and —"

"I'll t-t see you tomorrow, Jack," Mr. Liss called from the doorway. Then he winked at me.

The most evil wink I ever saw.

Because I knew what he meant. He didn't mean, *I'll see you tomorrow.* He meant, *You won't get away from me.*

He meant, *I'll see you in school and I'll hug you the way the alien hugged me.*

And then the alien will spread to you too. And then you'll hug everyone you meet. And the alien will spread to everyone in town!

I stood hugging myself in the middle of the living room. Trying to stop my whole body from trembling. I watched Mom talk quietly to Mr. Liss at the front door.

Don't let him touch you, I silently ordered her. *Don't shake hands with him. Don't touch him!*

I knew they were talking about me. They kept glancing quickly at me as they spoke.

Mom shrugged. Mr. Liss smiled reassuringly.

And then — finally — he left.

I heard a noise. Turned. And saw Billie waving wildly to me from the top of the stairs. "Jack, hurry! There are more aliens up here!" she called down. "I saw *ten* of them! No. A *hundred*!"

I growled and shook my fist at her. "Shut up! Shut up! This isn't a joke, Billie!"

Mom turned back to me. "Don't say another word," she said sharply. "I'm going to call Dr. Bendix. Maybe he'll see you *and* your sister."

She sighed. "I just hope Billie doesn't have to have her tonsils out."

She strode past me, heading to the kitchen phone. "Go upstairs and lie down for a bit," she instructed. "We can have a long talk about all this alien nonsense when your dad gets home."

"Will you *listen* to me then?" I demanded.

"Yes. But don't scare your sister with any more crazy stories." She disappeared into the kitchen.

Crazy stories?

Crazy stories?

Yes. It was a crazy story. But it was also true.

And it wasn't finished.

An alien creature had landed on Earth. The creature had hugged my teacher. Hugged him and then pushed its way into his back.

The alien had possessed my teacher.

And then it wanted to possess me too. It wanted to possess everyone!

My head spun from these terrifying thoughts. I could feel the blood pulsing at my temples.

What could I do? What?

I peered out the front window. And let out a startled cry.

Mr. Liss — he was still out there. On the curb in front of my house. *He was hugging the mailman!*

After a few seconds, Mr. Liss stepped back.

I saw green bubbles pop out from the mailman's ears.

Mr. Liss hurried away, smiling.

The mailman scratched one shoulder, then the next. He had a very bewildered expression on his face. The bubbles slid back into his ears. He shifted his mailbag and began shuffling heavily to the next house.

Now the mailman is going to start hugging people, I realized, gripped with horror. He will go from house to house, spreading the alien to everyone in the neighborhood.

I've got to *do* something, I realized. Fast!

But what?

Suddenly I had an idea.

Mr. Fleshman!

My neighbor. My *strange* neighbor.

Why hadn't I thought of him? I was so swept up in my own panic that I forgot the one person who could help!

Mr. Fleshman told me that he is a special-effects man for the movies. He has all kinds of mechanical monsters and ghosts in his house.

But that was just a cover-up.

One day, I was outside his house. I overheard Mr. Fleshman on the phone. He was talking to his boss. He said he was ready for the invasion. He said he could handle it.

That day, I realized that Mr. Fleshman was a government agent. He was preparing for the alien invasion. He promised his boss he would destroy the aliens when they landed.

Now the time had come. An alien had landed.

But did Mr. Fleshman know it?

I had to tell him. He was the only one who could help. The only one who would believe me. The only one who could stop the alien before it possessed everyone in L.A.!

Mom was still on the phone in the kitchen. I crept out the front door. Then ran as fast as I could along the fence that separates our two yards, up to Mr. Fleshman's back porch.

"Mr. Fleshman! Are you home?" I pounded on the kitchen door with both fists.

The door slid open.

"Mr. Fleshman? It's me — Jack! Mr. Fleshman?" My voice came out high and shrill.

I poked my head inside. "Emergency!" I shouted. "Mr. Fleshman — they landed! Are you home?"

No reply.

Maybe he's in the front of the house, I thought. Maybe he's in one of his workshops and can't hear me.

I pushed the back door open wider — and crept inside.

Fading afternoon sunlight washed into the kitchen from the window. I waited for my eyes to adjust to the dim light.

No signs of life in the kitchen. A cornflakes box

stood beside an empty bowl on the table. A pile of unopened mail was stacked on the counter.

The floor squeaked beneath my shoes as I made my way into the long back hall. "Mr. Fleshman?" I called. "Are you home?"

Silence.

From somewhere in the back of the house, I heard a soft rumble of music. Organ music, low and eerie.

"Mr. Fleshman — it's me — Jack!" I called.

I peeked into the den. Newspapers piled on the floor. A grinning skull on the bookshelf.

The house was full of skulls, and ghosts, and monsters. They were all props that Mr. Fleshman uses to make people think he works in the movies.

But I knew better.

The organ music rumbled louder. "Mr. Fleshman —?" I called again, cupping my hands around my mouth to be heard over the pounding chords.

I bumped into a low table against the wall. I cried out and jumped back.

And saw the photo album. The album I found the last time I went exploring in this big, frightening house.

I reached down and pulled the album open. I flipped through the pages. "Yes," I murmured. "I knew it."

I stared at photo after photo of green space aliens. Mr. Fleshman told me they were models he had built for a movie. But he was lying.

37

The creatures in these photos looked just like the alien that had pushed itself into Mr. Liss.

This proves it, I told myself. This proves that Mr. Fleshman is a government agent.

I was still holding the album as a figure stepped quickly from the shadows. "Mr. Fleshman —!" I cried.

He was dressed all in black, as usual. His cold silvery eyes moved from me to the photo album.

Then he turned back to me, studying me intently. "Jack," he said finally in his hoarse, whispery voice. "What are you doing here?"

"It — landed!" I cried.

His expression didn't change.

"An alien creature," I told him. "It landed. I saw it. It tried to hug me. It looked just like the creatures in this photo album."

He frowned. "I guess you've found out my little secret."

"Y-yes," I stammered. I slammed the album shut and dropped it back on the table.

"I know you're a government agent," I blurted out. "I didn't mean to eavesdrop, Mr. Fleshman. But I heard you on the phone."

He narrowed his silver eyes but didn't say anything. He seemed to be thinking hard. I guess he was trying to decide how much he could tell me.

"Are you with the FBI?" I asked.

He shook his head. "This is all between you and me, Jack," he said, leaning close. "You have to swear not to tell a soul. I'm a special agent. I'm with the Alien Detection Bureau."

"I knew it!" I cried.

He raised a finger to his lips, signaling for me to be silent.

"I'm trusting you, Jack. I'm trusting you not to reveal my secret. Not to anyone. Not even your parents."

"I won't tell anyone. I swear," I said, raising my right hand.

"There are more of them on the way, Jack," he revealed. "We got advance word that these creatures were going to land here. I've been setting up my headquarters. Waiting for them. My agents are on Red Alert."

"He — he hugged my science teacher!" I cried. "And my science teacher hugged the mailman. And — and —"

Mr. Fleshman placed a calming hand on my shoulder. "Don't worry, Jack. It's under control. We can handle them."

"But what are you going to do?" I demanded.

He raised a finger to his lips again. "Go home, Jack. Stay calm. Lock your doors and stay calm, okay?"

"Okay," I replied. "But —"

He began walking me to the kitchen door. "Don't tell anyone. Don't spread the panic. Keep yourself safe."

"Okay," I agreed.

He stopped at the back door and turned to me. "You are the only other person besides my agents who knows about this invasion," he said in a whisper. "Do you want to help us?"

"Of course!" I replied.

"Start a list," he instructed. "Start a list for me of everyone you see who gets invaded by these aliens."

"Just write down their names?" I asked.

He nodded solemnly. "It will be a big help. After we defeat them, I'll need that list."

I swallowed. "Okay. I'll start it right away."

"Don't put yourself in danger," Mr. Fleshman warned. "I know you. I know how you like to spy on people." He smiled. "You've been spying on *me* ever since I moved here!"

"Sorry," I muttered.

"Don't take any risks," he repeated. "If you see someone get hugged, write down the name. That's all. Keep yourself safe. I will take care of the rest."

"I'll be careful," I promised. "And I'll do my job."

"Don't worry," Mr. Fleshman said softly, calmly. "My agents and I will handle these creatures. No problem."

"I hope so," I murmured. I turned and ran home as fast as I could.

But I stopped in the middle of the front yard. Four kids from my class — Marsha Wiener,

Maddy James, Henry, and Derek — stood waiting for me by the front door.

"Hey, we just saw Mr. Liss!" Derek cried.

"Oh, noooo," I moaned.

The four of them moved quickly across the grass toward me. "What's wrong, Jack?" Maddy asked.

"Did he — did he *hug* you?" I stammered.

The two girls laughed. Henry and Derek squinted hard at me.

"Did he *what*?" Marsha demanded.

"Did he hug you?" I repeated in a trembling voice.

Marsha and Maddy exchanged glances.

They all moved closer.

"Yes, he hugged us," Derek said softly.

I gasped. "Stay away — please!" I pleaded.

Too late.

Derek and Henry surrounded me.

And then they both started to hug me.

8

"No —!"

I struggled to pull away. But Henry and Derek are *big* guys. Big and athletic. I couldn't free myself.

"Please —!" I begged.

They both lowered their arms and dropped back. Derek fell onto his back on the grass, laughing a shrill hyena laugh.

Henry collapsed to his knees beside him. He gleefully slapped Derek a high five.

I opened my mouth, but no sound came out.

"You are definitely weird," Derek said to me.

"Why would Mr. Liss hug us?" Henry demanded.

"What is your problem, Jack?" Marsha cried. "Why are you acting so weird?"

I backed up shakily and studied all four of them.

42

They weren't clicking their tongues. No green bubblegum bubbles blowing out of their ears.

"He — he didn't hug you?" I repeated.

Marsha laughed again. "We saw him at the corner. We waved to him. That's all."

"We came to see if you are okay," Maddy added. "You ran out of school so fast."

"I'm not okay!" I cried. "An alien creature —"

I stopped. They weren't listening to me. Marsha's mom was shouting to Marsha from their house across the street.

"I've got to go," Marsha said. "Anyone coming to my house?"

"Derek and I have to talk to Jack," Henry replied.

The two girls said good-bye and trotted across the street.

I led Derek and Henry into the house.

They walked into the living room and tossed their backpacks on the floor.

"I brought you the homework from Mrs. Hoff," Derek said. "You ran out so fast —"

"Forget the homework," I cut in. "You won't believe what happened. That space object you thought was a ball?"

"Yeah. Sorry we tossed it around," Henry said. "We only did it as a joke."

"Never mind that!" I cried. "Listen to me, guys. Let me finish! It wasn't a ball or a meteor. It was an alien spacecraft."

They both stared hard at me. Henry licked his bright blue braces.

"I had it on my dresser, and an alien creature climbed out," I told them. I couldn't wait to get the whole story out. I told them the whole thing without taking a breath.

I told them how the alien grew. How evil it looked. How it chased after me. How it hugged Mr. Liss and disappeared inside him. How Mr. Liss tried to hug me to spread the alien creature into me. How my mom walked in at just the right minute. How I saw Mr. Liss hugging the mailman.

I told them everything — except the part about Mr. Fleshman. And my assignment to keep a list of names. I'd promised Mr. Fleshman I wouldn't tell anyone about him.

I talked for ten minutes straight. By the time I finished, I was gasping for breath.

Henry and Derek continued to stare at me. They didn't reply. Didn't say a word.

Then a grin spread across Henry's face. "Saucerman strikes again!" he exclaimed.

"Jack, you need a reality check!" Derek said.

"But what I told you is real!" I protested. "You don't believe me about —"

"No, we don't," Henry interrupted. "Do we *ever* believe you? No." He picked up a couch pillow and began tossing it from hand to hand. Then he smashed the pillow into Derek's face.

Derek grabbed the pillow and hit Henry over the head with it.

"Give me a break!" I cried. "An alien from another planet has landed right here, and you guys think it's a joke!"

"We think *you're* a joke," Derek shot back.

"Then why did you come to my house?" I demanded.

"We told you. To apologize," Henry said. He shoved the pillow into Derek's face. Derek tried to grab it away, and missed.

"Are you going to try out for the swim team?" Derek asked.

Henry tried to smash him with the pillow. Derek ducked away. Then he messed up Henry's hair with both hands.

"Huh? The swim team?" I stared at them. "How can you think about the swim team now? There's an alien creature inside Mr. Liss, and it's spreading itself —"

"You're crazy. But we really need you on the team," Derek said.

"You know you're a terrific swimmer," Henry added. "At camp this summer, you were faster than anyone. You even beat some of the counselors."

"We really need you this year, Jack," Derek repeated. "Coach told us to *make* you try out."

"But, guys —" I started. I stopped myself. No

way they were going to listen to me. No way they were going to believe me.

"Okay. I'll try out." I lied to them — because there was no way I was going back to school.

How could I go back, knowing that Mr. Liss was possessed by an alien creature? Knowing that he was *waiting* for me there?

The next morning, I tried the old stomachache routine. But Mom made me go to school anyway. She said that my classes would take my mind off my stomach.

I walked to school as slowly as I could. Kids hurried past me. Marsha and Maddy waved to me as they rolled past on their bikes.

They all seem so happy, I thought. So normal.

If only they knew. . . .

By the time I arrived at school, I really *did* have a stomachache. Every muscle felt tight and tense.

My dread was weighing me down. I felt as if I weighed a thousand pounds!

I made my way to my locker and hung up my jacket. I pulled some textbooks off the top shelf and stuffed them into my backpack.

I glanced up at the hallway clock. It was late. The bell was about to ring.

I trudged down the long hall and turned the corner.

Could I get to Mrs. Hoff's room without running into Mr. Liss?

No.

The science teacher stood outside his classroom doorway. The ceiling light made his glasses glow, and a wide smile spread over his face when he saw me.

"Jack," he called, motioning to me. "Jack, t-t come here!"

froze. A frightened gasp escaped my throat.

Mr. Liss waved me over excitedly. "Come over here, Jack. Don't be afraid."

"Uh . . ." I stared at him, my heart pounding. My legs trembling, I took a step back.

"Jack —" the science teacher called, motioning frantically with both hands now. "Jack —!"

I turned and ran.

I had to escape from him. And I had to warn everyone else.

My backpack bounced heavily on my shoulders as I ran. Was Mr. Liss chasing after me? I didn't look back.

Mrs. Berkman's office came up in front of me. She is the middle-school principal.

I skidded to a stop and darted into the office. "I

have to see Mrs. Berkman!" I called breathlessly to the secretary.

I didn't give her a chance to reply. I spotted Mrs. Berkman standing beside her desk in the back office.

"Hey, wait —" the secretary cried.

But I bolted for the back office. "Mrs. Berkman — you've got to help me! You've got to listen to me!" I gasped.

Mrs. Berkman is short and thin and has bouncy blond hair and pale blue eyes. She dresses in sweaters and slacks and looks much too young to be a school principal.

She dropped the papers she was reading and narrowed her blue eyes at me. "Jack?"

"Please —" I begged. "This is important. I — I —" I didn't know where to start.

Mrs. Berkman stepped around me and closed the office door. She motioned for me to sit down in the chair across from her. Then she took her place behind the big, cluttered desk.

"Take a deep breath, Jack," she said softly. "Then tell me what's wrong."

I took a deep breath. But it didn't help. It didn't slow down my racing heart. It didn't stop me from shaking all over.

"It's a long story," I started, my voice cracking, my mouth so dry. "A space alien landed on Earth. It was in my room —"

"I heard you had a problem about that in class,"

Mrs. Berkman interrupted. She leaned toward me across the desk, tugging at the sleeves of her blue sweater, her eyes locked on mine. "Mrs. Hoff had to take you to the nurse?"

I nodded impatiently. "Yes, yes. But that's not important. You see, the alien hugged Mr. Liss. It went inside his back. It's inside him now!"

"Whoa." Mrs. Berkman climbed to her feet. The desk chair rolled back against the wall. "Take it slow, Jack. I'm not getting this."

She stepped around the side of her desk. "Are you telling me the plot of some science-fiction movie? Something you saw on TV?"

"No!" I cried. "Please. Please believe me."

I jumped to my feet too. "You've got to warn everyone!" I told her. "It — it's dangerous! It was so big and horrible looking. It's inside Mr. Liss, and it wants to get inside everyone! You've got to tell the police, or the FBI, or the president — or someone! Please, Mrs. Berkman — I'm begging you! Please!"

She studied me for a long moment.

"Do you believe me?" I cried, my voice high and shrill. "Do you?"

She frowned, her eyes still on me. "I see you're upset, Jack. But I don't know what to think. Why did this alien creature invade Mr. Liss? When did it happen? Where? In school?"

I took a deep breath. "In my house. The alien came here in a round spacecraft. It was in my room. It — it started to grow. The creature was green. It looked like a lizard. But it got bigger and bigger. And Mr. Liss came to my house."

"When?" the principal asked.

"Yesterday afternoon. Mr. Liss came to my house. The creature hugged him, harder and harder. And then —"

I choked. My mouth was so dry. The words caught in my throat.

"Please —" I whispered. "Believe me."

Mrs. Berkman moved around the desk toward me. "I do believe you, Jack," she said softly. "I can see that you're telling the truth."

"You *do*?" I squeaked. Finally! Finally, someone believed me!

"You poor guy," Mrs. Berkman said. She put her hands on my shoulders. Green bubbles poked out of her ears.

"You're so t-t-t upset, you're trembling, Jack. Come here. T-t. Let me give you a hug."

51

10

Her hands slid around me.

"No —!" I uttered a cry and jerked back. I stumbled over the chair, backed away until I bumped against the wall. A picture frame clattered to the floor. The glass shattered loudly.

"Come here, Jack." The principal stepped over the broken glass, her arms outstretched. "Don't be afraid."

"You — you talked to Mr. Liss this morning?" I choked out, moving sideways toward the office door.

Mrs. Berkman nodded. A strange smile crossed her face. Her pale eyes appeared to roll in her head. She clicked her tongue several times.

"Mr. Liss and I had a nice talk before the students started to arrive," she said. "He's such a nice man. T-t."

"He — he *hugged* you!" I accused. I slid another step closer to the door.

She nodded again, her blond hair bouncing on top of her head. She stretched out her hands. Long silver nails shot out from her fingers. "It doesn't hurt, Jack," she whispered. "You want to be one of us — don't you?"

"No!" I screamed. "No way! I don't! I want to be me!"

She kicked a triangle of glass out of her way. "We need your body, Jack. We need a lot of bodies. T-t-t." Green bubbles bobbed from her ears.

I slid along the wall, just a few feet from the door now.

"One hug, Jack," she insisted. The long nails made a metallic sound as she clicked them together. "It doesn't hurt. You will hardly feel it."

"No —" I choked out. "No —"

Her smile faded. Her eyes grew cold. "You know too much. We can't have you telling people about us — not until the others arrive. Not until we are ready."

She dove at me.

I spun to the door. Grabbed the handle. Tugged it open.

Then I burst out into the hall — and ran straight into Mr. Liss.

"Here you are!" he cried, wrapping his arms around my waist.

broke away from him too. And took off down the long, empty front hall. My shoes thudded on the hard floor.

I realized I'd left my backpack in the principal's office. No way I'd ever go back for it.

I glanced back and saw Mr. Liss and Mrs. Berkman trotting side by side down the hall, coming after me.

They are the first two names on my list, I thought.

I wondered if Mr. Fleshman had already started to fight the invasion. I wondered if I should tell him the alien was spreading itself through the school.

You know too much. The principal's cold words flashed once again through my mind. *You know too much.*

Yes, I did. I did know too much. I knew exactly what was going on.

And I was the only one who knew it.

I turned the corner. Which way now? Which way?

How could I get away from them?

I had to hide. I had to find a place where I'd be safe, where I could think.

A bunch of kids looked up as I ran past the library. I heard a girl call my name, but I didn't stop.

No place to hide in the library.

I glanced behind me. And saw Mr. Liss and Mrs. Berkman turn the corner.

I took a deep breath and began to run harder. Two teachers leaned over a water fountain at the end of the hall. "What is the assembly today?" I heard one of them ask.

"Two policemen," the other teacher replied. "Talking about law enforcement or something."

Great! I thought.

Policemen — coming to our school. That's perfect. I'll be able to tell them everything. The police will be able to capture Mr. Liss and Mrs. Berkman before they can hug anyone else.

The two teachers looked up in surprise as I hurtled past them. "Hey — slow down!" one of them called.

I had to lose Mr. Liss and Mrs. Berkman. I couldn't let them see me go into the auditorium.

I'll run up to the second floor, then back down, I decided.

I flew down the length of the hall, past the music room, past the art room and the science labs. Then I ran back downstairs on the other stairway.

Into the back of the auditorium. The stage was brightly lighted, but the seats stood in darkness. No one in here yet. My wheezing breaths echoed loudly over the vast room.

"Who's there?" someone called from the stage.

I ducked into the deep shadow along the auditorium wall.

Two men in gray overalls were setting up the microphones for the assembly. They squinted out into the auditorium, searching for me.

I pressed my back against the wall and held my breath.

Did they see me? No. Muttering to each other, they returned to work. "Testing. One-two —? This thing isn't even on!" one of them declared.

I let out a sigh and searched for a place to hide. I decided just to duck down low in a seat near the back where it was really dark.

A few minutes later, the auditorium doors all opened. Kids began streaming in, talking loudly, laughing, pushing, goofing around.

Everyone likes assemblies. They're usually boring. But it means no class for at least an hour or so.

As the rows started to fill, I jumped up and

joined a bunch of kids who were heading toward the middle of the auditorium. Across the seats, I saw Marsha and Maddy waving to me.

But I didn't join them. I didn't want to sit with my class. That's the first place Mr. Liss and Mrs. Berkman would look.

I moved into a row with a bunch of eighth graders and hunched down low in my seat, so low that I couldn't be seen from the stage.

I kept darting my eyes left and right, from aisle to aisle, watching for Mr. Liss and Mrs. Berkman. I kept myself tense and ready. If they came down an aisle looking for me, I would scramble away in the other aisle.

I couldn't wait for the assembly to begin. It seemed as if I'd already been hiding in the auditorium for hours.

As I waited, I tried to think of the best way to tell my story to the police officers. I had to tell it quickly. Simply. I had to make sense. I couldn't let my panic tangle me up.

I had to make the officers believe me.

I gasped when I saw Mrs. Berkman making her way down the left aisle. I leaned forward, preparing to make my escape.

But she was talking to two girls from the cheerleading squad. She walked right past my aisle and didn't see me.

I let out a long whoosh of air. Leaning against

the seat in front of me, I watched her climb up the stairway at the side of the stage and stride to the podium.

My hands felt icy and wet. My stomach was a hard knot.

I silently rehearsed over and over what I would say to the policemen. I pictured the police capturing Mr. Liss and Mrs. Berkman and leading them away.

And then what? I wondered.

What would happen to them after they were arrested?

Would they be arrested? Was it a crime to be possessed by a space alien?

Questions. Too many questions.

I couldn't answer any of them. I only knew one thing — it was up to me to save everyone in school.

I let out another long sigh as the two black-uniformed officers finally stepped onto the stage. Mrs. Berkman moved quickly to greet them. They all shook hands.

The officers sat down on folding chairs beside the podium. Mrs. Berkman moved to the microphone. "Is this t-t-t on?" The speakers squealed. Kids laughed and held their ears.

"It's too loud," Mrs. Berkman said. She tapped the microphone a few times. "There. That's better. Quiet, please, people. Quiet."

Silence fell over the auditorium. I leaned forward. Prepared to move.

A yellow spotlight traveled across the stage and finally found Mrs. Berkman. "We are very lucky today," she began, "to have two officers t-t from the Los Angeles Police Department here to speak to us."

As she continued her introduction, I crept out of my seat and pushed my way along the row of eighth graders. "Where are you going?" someone asked. I didn't reply.

"Ow!" A girl cried out when I stepped on her foot.

"Sorry," I muttered. I made my way to the aisle.

"It gives me great pleasure to turn over the stage to Officer Munroe and Officer Tunney," Mrs. Berkman announced.

She stepped back as the two policemen stood up. The auditorium rang out with applause.

I waited until the applause died down.

And then I took off, running to the stage.

As I ran, I waved my hands wildly above my head. "Stop!" I cried. "Stop everything! You have to stop! Please — listen to me! The school — it's been invaded by aliens!"

12

I heard kids gasp. Some kids laughed.

"Archer — what are you *doing*?" a boy called.

"There goes Saucerman," someone muttered.

I heard kids murmuring and whispering in surprise.

I didn't care. "I'm telling the truth!" I called up to the officers breathlessly. "Please — you've *got* to listen to me!"

The auditorium erupted in startled cries and laughter.

"Sit down!" someone shouted.

"Who *is* that?" I heard a teacher cry out.

"Go, Jack!" a boy called. Several kids laughed.

"Please —!" I choked out. I saw the two officers step back. Saw the surprise on their faces. Saw their bodies tense.

I reached the stairs at the side of the stage. "I have to . . . tell you about the alien!" I gasped.

I stumbled on the steps. Banged my knee hard.

I heard a roar of laughter behind me.

Pain shot up my leg. The knee throbbed. I staggered onto the stage.

The officers squinted into the stage light at me.

"I have to tell you —" I started. My heart pounded so hard, I could barely breathe.

Mrs. Berkman moved quickly to block my path. As she stepped in front of me, she forced a smile onto her face.

"Please —!" I called over her shoulder to the two police officers.

But Mrs. Berkman took me by both arms. "It's okay, Jack," she said, shouting over the murmurs and cries of the kids from the seats. "It's okay."

"No —!" I protested.

She grasped my shoulders and gently moved me back. "A troubled student," she called to the officers. "I'm so sorry. I can deal with him."

The officers nodded.

A hush fell quickly over the auditorium.

Mrs. Berkman wrapped her arms around me and forced me to the side of the stage. "Please continue," she called back to the policemen.

"Let me go —" I protested.

"It's okay, Jack," she repeated in a whisper. "It's going to be okay."

She moved me behind one of the curtains, out

of view of the stage. "Okay," she whispered. "Okay."

Then she wrapped her arms around me. Wrapped me in a hug. Tighter.

Tighter . . .

I heard the long, sharp nails shoot out from her fingers.

"Oh."

I let out a gasp of pain as I felt them pressing into my back.

13

"Ohhhh." A horrified moan escaped my throat.

Coldness. A wash of cold swept over my back. Cold and sharp as an icicle.

Ten icicles.

The sharp cold stabbed deeper.

No, I told myself. Don't let her do it. Don't let the alien in.

I sucked in air, thinking hard, struggling to think over my panic, over the spreading cold.

And then I shut my eyes. Let my knees fold.

I pretended to faint.

I slumped hard to the floor. My arms collapsed under me.

I heard Mrs. Berkman cry out in surprise.

The painful coldness faded instantly.

She stood over me, staring down with her

mouth open. Before she could move, I rolled over. Jumped up. Spun away from her.

Her eyes bulged in surprise. She grabbed for me with both hands.

But I took off running. Behind the curtain. Into a maze of backstage curtains, and boxes, and stage props.

I could hear the scrape of her footsteps as she came after me. Beyond the curtains, I could hear the droning voice of one of the officers. He was interrupted by applause. And then he continued to talk.

I have to talk to them! I told myself. I have to let them know about Mr. Liss and Mrs. Berkman.

But how?

If I ran back onstage, Mrs. Berkman would grab me before I got a word out.

I ducked behind a backdrop and crept along the back wall of the auditorium.

"Jack — where are you?" Mrs. Berkman called softly. "It'll be okay, Jack. It doesn't hurt. You'll see."

I stopped. The curtain fluttered. The principal was moving quickly along the other side of it.

Hide, Jack, I ordered myself. Hide.

My eyes searched around frantically. A stack of boxes near the back door. No. She'd find me easily back there.

"Jack — where are you? You can't hide from me." She was closer.

64

I spun back and trotted in the direction I'd come. And saw a large, dust-covered trunk just in front of the curtain.

Was it empty?

I lifted the lid and peered inside.

Yuck!

The sharp, sour odor of mothballs swept over me. Mothballs and mildew. The trunk was filled with rotting old costumes.

I covered my mouth. My stomach lurched. The smell was so powerful, I felt sick!

"Jack — don't try to hide," Mrs. Berkman called. Closer now. Seconds away from finding me. From catching me.

I hesitated for another moment, sickened by the sour smell from the trunk.

I had no choice. No choice.

My whole body trembling, I climbed over the side of the old trunk — and scrambled inside.

"Jack? Jack?" I heard her whispered call as I lowered the lid over me.

Had she seen me?

I huddled in the darkness, hugging myself. Holding my breath.

But the sickening smell invaded my nose and mouth.

I . . . I can't breathe in here, I thought, starting to panic. I never smelled anything this bad!

The footsteps, sharp and rapid, nearly made me leap up.

But they moved on quickly. Mrs. Berkman walked right past me.

I breathed a silent sigh. My stomach lurched again. I swallowed, once, twice, struggling to keep my breakfast down. And I shut my eyes and listened.

The other officer was talking now. I could hear clearly. He was answering questions from the audience.

Slowly, carefully, I poked up the trunk lid and peered out. To my surprise, I could see the front of the stage.

I could see the officer, tall and lanky, leaning over the podium, his mouth close to the microphone. And I could see his partner sitting with his legs crossed on the folding chair.

I'll wait in this disgusting trunk, I decided.

Maybe I can make it until the assembly is over, until the officers are walking off. Then I'll jump out and tell them my story.

Sweat poured down my forehead. My stomach churned. I held my nose and breathed through my mouth.

I'll never get this sick smell off me, I thought. I'll smell it for the rest of my life.

I kept the lid raised less than an inch and peered out to the front of the stage. Finally, the officer stepped away from the podium and joined his partner. Applause rang out. The assembly was over.

I swallowed hard and raised both hands up to the trunk lid. I prepared to jump out.

At the podium, Mrs. Berkman thanked the officers. She instructed the kids in the audience to go quickly and quietly to their next classes.

Then she led the policemen off the stage. Toward me. A few feet in front of my trunk.

"Thank you so much," I heard her say. "You were both wonderful."

Pushing up the heavy wooden lid, I stared in horror as the principal hugged them. First the tall, lanky one. Then his partner.

I saw them gasp in surprise as Mrs. Berkman wrapped her arms around them. And held them, pressing tighter. Tighter. The long nails slid out. She shoved them deep into the officers' backs.

Slowly, as the alien invaded them, their startled expressions faded.

"T-t-t. We always enjoy speaking to students," the lanky officer said to Mrs. Berkman. Green bubbles bulged from his ears.

Mrs. Berkman flashed him a pleased grin.

"They asked such t-t intelligent questions," the other policeman commented. He scratched one shoulder, then the other. Then he made loud kissing sounds with his lips.

I lowered the lid and sank wearily into the trunk.

I don't believe this! I thought.

She got both of them! The alien has invaded both policemen too.

I'll have to add them to the list, I told myself. I struggled to remember their names.

What will they do now? I wondered. Spread it to the whole police department?

I have to get home, I told myself. More and more people are being possessed by the alien. I have to tell Mr. Fleshman. I have to make sure that he and his agents know what's happening.

I waited until the officers and Mrs. Berkman were gone and the auditorium had cleared out. Then I struggled out of the foul, disgusting trunk.

I mopped the sweat from my face and took several deep breaths, sucking in fresh air.

"I have to get out of here," I murmured out loud.

I made my way to the back of the auditorium. I stepped into the hall and started toward the door.

And two kids grabbed me roughly by the arms.

"Henry!" I cried. "Derek!"

"You're coming with us," Derek insisted.

"Why? Where are you taking me?" I cried. "Where?"

enry giggled. "What's your problem, Jack?"

"Just come with us," Derek ordered.

They dragged me around the corner and then through a door halfway down the hall. "The locker room?" I cried. "What's going on? What do you want?"

They both let go of me as another figure stepped out from behind a row of lockers.

"Here he is, Coach Finney," Derek declared. "We found him."

"He forgot all about tryouts," Henry told the coach.

Coach Finney frowned at me as he walked over to us. He wore a sleeveless T-shirt over baggy black swim trunks. He is a young guy, nearly as short as I am, but very athletic looking, with a broad chest and bulging biceps.

Coach Finney has pale blue eyes and wavy black hair that he pulls back in a ponytail. A lot of girls think he's really cute. I know that both Marsha and Maddy have crushes on him.

"You forgot about tryouts?" he asked, narrowing those pale blue eyes at me. "You sure you want to be on the swim team?"

Henry and Derek both watched me.

"Yes, I really do," I told the coach. "But I'm kind of in a hurry right now. Do you think —"

Coach Finney laughed. "A hurry?" He glanced at his watch. "I'll write you a pass to your next class."

"But — but —" I sputtered. How could I try out for the swim team while an alien creature was taking over the school? Maybe taking over all of L.A.!

"Get changed," Coach Finney ordered. "There are swimsuits in that cabinet if you didn't bring one. Try to find one that won't fall off in the water. I take off ten points for that!"

He laughed. Henry and Derek laughed too.

I swallowed hard. I didn't feel like swimming. I had to get away from there. I had to get help.

I thought about just taking off. Running away and explaining later. But I knew Henry and Derek wouldn't let me get away.

I'll get the tryout over with quickly, I decided. Then I'll hurry to Mr. Fleshman's house.

"Meet you at the pool," Coach Finney said. He vanished behind the row of lockers.

"Hurry up," Henry urged.

"You can do it!" Derek declared. He slapped me a high five.

I'll do it and get it over with, I decided.

I stepped over to the cabinet and found a suit that looked my size. I carried it over to an empty locker and started to change.

A few minutes later, I opened the door to the swimming pool. A burst of hot air and chlorine washed over me.

Coach Finney sat hunched on the diving board, scribbling on a clipboard. I saw four other guys who had come to try out. They were already in the pool, doing slow warm-up laps.

Henry and Derek sat cross-legged on the tile floor at the edge of the pool. Their swimsuits were totally dry.

That's weird, I thought. Usually, you can't keep those two out of the water. I know they don't have to try out because they're the team captains.

But why aren't they going in the pool?

Henry flashed me a thumbs-up. Derek made swimming motions with both arms. "Good luck!" he called.

"Thanks!" I called out to him. I lowered myself into the warm water. As I began to take a few warm-up laps, I could feel how tense and tight my muscles were.

The warm water felt soothing. I dove under the surface and swam across the pool underwater.

When I came up, Coach Finney was blowing his whistle. The five of us swam up to the diving board.

"I was going to do individual, timed tryouts," the coach announced, tugging his ponytail free of the whistle chain. "But why don't we speed things up? Let's have a race. All five of you."

Several groans rose up from the pool. My eyes went from swimmer to swimmer. I knew all of these kids. But I didn't know if they were good swimmers or not. I wondered if any of them were as fast as me.

"Climb out," Coach Finney instructed. "I want to see a racing dive from this side, then race two complete laps."

We climbed out, dripping and shaking water off like dogs.

Coach Finney turned to Henry and Derek. "How about it? Join the race, guys. Give them something to compete against."

I saw Henry and Derek exchange quick glances. What was that expression on their faces? Fear?

No, Jack, you're imagining that, I told myself.

"Uh . . . I can't swim today, Coach," Henry murmured, keeping his eyes down on the tiles. "I have a cold or something."

"I can't, either," Derek said. "I've got an ear infection."

Weird, I thought. That's not like them at all.

But I didn't have time to think about it. Coach Finney blew his whistle, and the race tryout was on.

I got off to a bad start. My racing dive was awkward, and I landed far behind the others. I worked to catch up, pacing myself, moving steadily but slowly at first. Then I picked up speed and swam full out on the last lap.

I was breathing hard as I neared the finish. But it felt good. I was swimming smoothly, faster than I ever had. Maybe all the fear and excitement of the morning had me really wired. Maybe my muscles were happy to have the release.

I finished first, at least four or five strokes ahead of the next swimmer.

"Way to go, Jack!" Coach Finney cried. He moved to the edge to help pull me from the water. "Very impressive. We'll work on your dive. But you have a really good stroke."

Gasping for breath, I thanked him and turned to Henry and Derek. To my surprise, they weren't there.

Weird, I thought. They dragged me here. Couldn't they wait to watch me race?

Coach Finney tossed me a towel. I wrapped it around my shoulders and made my way to the locker room. As I walked, I could feel myself tensing up again.

The swimming had been a nice break. It even

took my mind off the space alien for a few minutes. But now all of the horror, all of my fear, came rushing back to me.

A chill rolled down my back as I stepped into the locker room. I moved quickly to my locker, drying myself as I walked.

"I've got to get out of this school," I murmured out loud.

I tossed the towel to the floor and pulled open the locker door.

"Hey!" I cried out as Henry and Derek burst out from behind the row of lockers. "You scared me!" I cried.

They both laughed.

"Where were you?" I demanded. "Did you see the race? Did you see me beat those other guys?"

They didn't reply.

Henry's smile faded. He stepped in front of me.

"What are you doing?" I cried. "What's your problem?"

Derek moved behind me.

I glanced back — and realized I was trapped between them.

"Hey —" I protested.

"It won't t-t-t hurt, Jack," Henry murmured. "Really. T-t. It won't hurt at all."

I couldn't move. I couldn't scream.

They raised their arms and closed in on me.

15

Uttering a loud groan, I pushed out with my elbows. Tried to duck down and squirm free.

But Henry and Derek are big guys. Strong and wide.

They closed in on me, holding me helpless. Clicking their tongues excitedly as they hugged me.

I'm doomed, I realized. I'm going to be invaded now. I'm going to be one of them.

"*What's going on?*" a voice bellowed.

"Huh?" The two boys gasped and stepped back.

Coach Finney strode up to the lockers, eyeing us suspiciously.

"We were just congratulating Jack," Derek declared. He patted me on the back.

"He's the man!" Henry exclaimed. "Derek and I knew he could do it!"

"Well, let him get dressed," Coach Finney ordered. "You two come with me. I want you to help me with something."

He led Henry and Derek away.

I breathed a sigh of relief. My hands were trembling so hard, I could barely get dressed.

Now I had two more names to add to my list.

Who got to my two friends? I wondered. Who hugged them?

Was it Mr. Liss? Mrs. Berkman? Someone else?

How many teachers were possessed by the alien? How many kids?

I pushed open the locker room door and peered up and down the hall. When I was certain no one was watching, I made a run for the door.

I kept expecting someone to yell, *Stop!* Or someone to block my path.

But I burst out the door, into a cloudy, hot afternoon. The air felt steamy and wet, as if I'd stepped back into the school swimming pool.

I took a deep breath and took off, running across the school grounds. Past the playground. Empty now. Past the teachers' parking lot.

Then I crossed the street and kept running. My leg muscles ached from my swim race. But I ignored the pain — and the light drizzle of rain that had started to fall.

I ran full speed. I had to stop at the next corner

as a big moving van rumbled past. Then I took off again.

A few minutes later, my house came into view.

Mom will be home, I realized.

Yes. Mom didn't go to work today, because Billie still wasn't feeling well.

If only I could get her to believe me, I thought. If only I could convince her that I'm not making up wild stories, that we're all in such danger.

I knew I had to make one more try.

I threw open the front door and went tearing through the hall. "Mom! Mom!" I screamed breathlessly. "Where are you? Mom?"

Silence.

I stopped at the back hallway. "Mom? Are you here?"

No reply.

I spun through the hall, peering into every room. Then I turned and ran to the front stairs. "Mom? Are you upstairs? I have to talk to you! Mom?"

I could hear a window blind slapping against a window. No other sound.

"Weird," I murmured.

I made my way to the kitchen, the only room I hadn't searched. "Mom?" I called out. "It's me! I —"

I stepped into the kitchen and let out a gasp.

What was that shiny stuff on the kitchen floor?

Shiny green puddles.

Green slime.

Clumps of green slime on the floor near the table.

"It was here!" I murmured.

The space creature was here.

I stared in horror at the green clumps on the floor.

Mom? Billie?

What happened to them?

What did it *do* to them?

16

I felt sick. My stomach lurched as I stared down at the green clumps on the floor. I stared at them until they became a green blur.

Then I raised my eyes and saw the note on the refrigerator.

"Huh?" I shook myself, as if trying to shake away my fear.

Mom always leaves notes for us on the refrigerator. This one was stuck under a smile-face magnet.

I tore it off the refrigerator door. The magnet bounced across the floor. I raised the note in my trembling hand and read the words in blue ink in Mom's neat, careful handwriting:

Jack — Billie's tonsils are acting up again. She couldn't even swallow her favorite, lime Jell-O.

79

Dad and I took her to the doctor. We'll call you when we can. Make yourself a peanut butter sandwich if we're not back in time for dinner.

Love, M

I read the note twice, holding it in both hands to keep it from shaking. Finally, I let it fall to the floor and uttered a long sigh.

"Wow," I murmured. "Poor Billie."

Would they take her to the hospital? Would the doctors take out her tonsils? I wondered if it hurts to have your tonsils removed.

I read the note one more time.

Lime Jell-O. Lime Jell-O . . .

"Oh, wow," I murmured. I dropped down to the floor beside the kitchen table. I pushed my finger into one of the shimmering green globs. Then I raised the finger. Sniffed it. Then licked it.

Yes. Lime Jell-O.

Not alien creature slime.

At least everyone is safe from the alien, I thought. For now.

I climbed to my feet and glanced around the kitchen. The breakfast dishes were still piled in the sink. Half a slice of toast sat on the counter beside an empty orange juice bottle.

I'm all alone here, I realized.

And if they took Billie to the hospital, I'll be all alone till late tonight.

A chill made me shudder. What if they come looking for me? Mr. Liss? Mrs. Berkman? Henry and Derek?

What if they come here for me?

How can I protect myself?

I'll follow Mr. Fleshman's advice, I decided. I'll lock the doors. If anyone comes to the door, I won't answer. I won't answer the door for anybody.

The doorbell rang.

"No!" I nearly jumped out of my skin.

I froze at the kitchen doorway.

The bell chimed again. And again.

"Jack — are you home?" a voice called. A girl's voice.

I made my way to the living room and peeked out the front window. Marsha and Maddy!

What do they want? I asked myself. Why are they here? School isn't out yet. What are they doing here?

The doorbell chimed again.

I moved to the door. But I didn't open it. "Wh-What do you want?" I stammered.

"Let us in!" Marsha pleaded.

"Jack — we're scared!" Maddy cried.

"Scared? Scared of what?" I asked through the door.

"Something very weird is going on at school," Maddy replied.

"We're scared, Jack," Marsha said. "We want to talk to you. Open the door — please!"

I stopped with my hand on the door handle.

Should I trust them?

Should I let them in?

I hooked the chain and pulled the front door open a crack.

"Jack — open up!" Maddy insisted.

I stared out at them, trying to see if they had been possessed. Maddy's frizzed-out black hair flew wildly around her head. Her blue eyes flashed excitedly.

Marsha's features were twisted in fright. Tiny beads of sweat glistened on her forehead beneath her red hair.

"What's wrong with you, Jack?" Maddy demanded. "Why won't you let us in?"

I hesitated. They weren't clicking their tongues. No green bubbles poked out of their ears.

"Do you want to hug me?" I asked.

Marsha laughed. Maddy scowled. "Of course

not!" Maddy declared. "Are you sick or something?"

I took off the chain and pulled open the door. The girls pushed past me into the house. Their backpacks bumped me as they hurried inside.

I followed them into the living room. I couldn't decide whether to tell them about the space alien or not. I didn't want to frighten them.

Besides, they probably wouldn't believe me anyway.

"What's wrong?" I asked them. "You both look really frightened."

"It's Henry and Derek," Maddy replied, glancing out the front window. "They were acting so strange."

Marsha shuddered. "I hope they didn't follow us."

"What did they do?" I asked.

"They were talking funny," Maddy replied, pushing down her frizzy hair with one hand. "They didn't sound like themselves at all."

"Did they try to hug you?" I asked. "Did they hug you?"

Marsha shivered again.

Maddy opened her mouth to answer. But a heavy *THUD* outside made all three of us jump.

"It's Henry and Derek!" Marsha gasped, raising her hands to her freckled cheeks. "They *did* follow us!"

Another hard *THUD* from the front yard made us run to the window.

Staring out, I saw something hit the trunk of the pine tree by the front walk and bounce onto the grass.

"A rock!" I cried.

A round orange rock. About the size of a softball.

Marsha and Maddy cried out as another orange ball crashed onto the driveway.

It's the invasion! I realized.

Mr. Fleshman told me that more aliens were on the way. And now here they were, crashing down onto the street and front yards. Bouncing to Earth in round orange balls that looked just like the one I'd found.

"I don't believe it!" I gasped. Despite my horror, I had to see them. I ran to the front, pulled open the door, and burst outside.

The two girls followed close behind.

My mouth dropped open in amazement as I watched the shower of orange rocks. Like an orange hailstorm — dozens and dozens of them — crashing onto our block.

My heart pounding, I turned to Marsha and Maddy. I expected to see expressions of fear and amazement on their faces.

I didn't expect to find them *smiling*!

"It's about t-t-t time they got here," Maddy said.

"Yeah. What kept them?" Marsha replied.

They both turned to me, eyes wide and glowing.

"Our friends have t-t arrived," Marsha said.

"Don't try to run, Jack," Maddy added. "You're outnumbered now."

18

"N o —!"

I let out a sharp cry — and spun away from them.

They both grabbed for me. But I had already started to run.

I dove back into the house — and slammed the front door.

I could hear them shrieking angrily as I struggled to lock it. I jammed the chain back into place.

"Let us in!" Maddy called.

They hammered on the door. Then the door shook against loud, heavy thuds.

BANG ... BANG ...

They're using their shoulders, I realized. They're trying to break the door down!

"You can't get away from us, Jack!" Maddy called in.

BANG . . . BANG . . .

"T-t-t. We're all here now!" Marsha cried breathlessly. "We're here and we're ready!"

"We need your t-t body, Jack!"

"It won't hurt. Really. It won't!"

"One hug. One quick hug. And you'll be one of us."

"Let us in!"

The door shook with another heavy *THUD*.

Would it hold? Would it keep them out?

I heard a crash overhead as an alien spacecraft hit the roof.

"The back door! Is it locked?" I cried out loud.

I was halfway to the kitchen when the phone rang.

"YAAAI!" I let out a startled scream. And grabbed the kitchen phone off the wall. "Hello?" I gasped.

"Jack?"

"Dad —!"

"Jack, I'm at the hospital," his voice rang in my ear. I struggled to hear him over my gasping breaths.

"Billie has to have her tonsils out," he told me. "Your mom and I are going to be here till late. Are you okay?"

"No, I'm not!" I cried frantically. Even from the back of the house, I could hear Marsha and Maddy pounding against the front door.

"What did you say?" Dad asked. "I can't hear

too well, Jack. It's very noisy in this reception room."

"I'm not okay!" I shrieked. "You've got to get help, Dad! Aliens from outer space are landing. Hundreds of them! Right in the front yard!"

I took a deep breath and waited for Dad's reply.

I could hear voices in the background and phones ringing.

Dad sighed heavily into the phone. "Jack," he said finally, "I'm ashamed of you."

"Huh?" I gasped.

"Your sister is in the hospital. This is not the time for your crazy stories," he snapped angrily.

"But, Dad —" I tried to protest.

"Do you think you can be a grown-up?" Dad continued. "Do you think you can drop the crazy flying saucer stuff and be responsible?"

"Dad, please!" I begged. "Marsha and Maddy are going to hug me! They're possessed, Dad! They —"

"Not another word," Dad cried angrily. "Listen to me, Jack. Do your homework. Make yourself something to eat. And stop acting so silly."

Silly?

I swallowed hard. I had to make him understand. I had to make him believe me.

Another spacecraft bounced on the roof. I heard it roll down the shingles and thud onto the grass outside the kitchen window.

I took a deep breath. "Dad — listen —" I started.

Silence on the other end of the line.

"Dad?"

He had hung up.

I tossed the phone down and hurried to the front window. I peered out at the front stoop. Marsha and Maddy had disappeared.

I breathed a sigh of relief. The front door had held, had kept them out.

But for how long?

I gazed down the front lawn to the street.

The air crackled with the sound of splitting rocks. It sounded like a hundred little firecrackers exploding. The spacecrafts were cracking open like eggs. The alien creatures — dozens and dozens of them — came crawling out.

Like green insects at first. The size of grasshoppers.

Then growing. Growing to resemble fat green lizards. Then growing even more. Growing so quickly.

Rising up on their hind legs. Teeth sliding from their widening jaws. Podlike feet slapping the ground and pavement. Slender arms lengthening, then bulging with enormous muscles. Four-fingered hands raking the air.

My face pressed to the window, I stared in horror as the creatures lumbered heavily over the

90

lawns and sidewalks. Their bulging eyes rolling beneath the hard shells that topped their heads, they staggered off in all directions.

Thick trails of slime poured off their shimmering bodies, puddling the grass.

My chest suddenly felt about to burst. I'd been holding my breath the whole time!

I let out a long whoosh of air and returned my gaze to the front lawn. The grass was littered with cracked orange rocks and piles of white slime.

The creatures were staggering away. Still growing, still stretching as they strode over the lawns.

They are spreading out, I realized. Spreading out over the whole neighborhood.

I could hear screams and loud cries from across the street. Dogs barked ferociously. I saw Mr. and Mrs. Anderson run out of their house, waving their arms frantically.

A police patrol car pulled up. Two black-uniformed officers jumped out.

The Andersons ran up to the police. They were waving their hands wildly, all talking at once. "Do something!" I heard Mr. Anderson scream. "Can't you *do* something?"

And then I watched the two officers step forward. They moved quickly. One policeman hugged Mr. Anderson. His partner hugged Mrs. Anderson.

I saw the long silver nails slide out. And I watched in horror as the policemen shoved the nails into my neighbors' backs.

The Andersons stood stunned for a moment. Then I watched them hurry off to hug someone else.

"The whole neighborhood . . ." I murmured to myself. "The whole neighborhood . . ."

Gripped in terror, I pressed my face against the window. Watching. Listening.

"Mr. Fleshman." I murmured his name out loud.

What was he doing about this? What was he doing to stop this invasion?

Was he out somewhere with his agents, preparing to fight them? How *could* he fight them? There were so many of them, and they were spreading quickly to everyone!

My list of names won't be very helpful if everyone in L.A. is possessed! I thought.

I started to the back door. Mr. Fleshman told me to stay home. But I couldn't. I had to find out what he was doing.

I reached to open the door — and the phone rang. My heart pounding, I grabbed it off the wall.

"Jack?"

"Dad?"

"Sorry we got cut off before, Jack. Have you calmed down? Are you okay?"

"No, Dad," I cried. "Dad — the whole neighborhood —! They've landed!"

"I can't hear you," he shouted. "We have a very bad connection. And it's so noisy here."

"Dad, please listen —" I begged.

"Your mom and I are going to get home very late. Can you put yourself to bed? We'll look in on you when we get home."

"But, Dad —"

"Billie is being operated on now," he said. "If it goes well, we may be able to bring her home tomorrow."

"That's good," I said. "But it isn't safe. The aliens —"

"You might have to get yourself to school in the morning," Dad said, shouting over the voices at the hospital. "Mom and I may leave for the hospital very early. We don't want Billie to wake up without us being there."

"I can't go back to that school," I said. I swallowed hard. "Dad, we have to talk as soon as you get home tonight."

"What did you say?" he asked. "I'd better go. Someone wants to use this phone. Bye, Jack."

The phone went silent. I dropped it back onto the wall.

I was shaking all over. "Why won't he *listen* to me?" I cried out loud.

I took a deep breath. I knew there was only one person who would listen. One person who knew what was happening. Mr. Fleshman.

I started to the door again — but stopped.

The aliens are running all over the neighborhood, I told myself. What if there's one waiting for me in the backyard? What if there are a *dozen* of them out there?

I turned and ran upstairs. From my bedroom windows, I could check out the yard. And I could look down at Mr. Fleshman's house and see if he was home.

I crossed my room to the window, pulled it open all the way, and shoved my head out.

My eyes quickly swept over the backyard. I could see the orange alien spacecrafts, cracked open like eggs, scattered over the grass. But no alien creatures.

Across the yard, I saw a light on at the side of Mr. Fleshman's house. I squinted into his window.

I could see him in there.

What was he doing?

Sitting in a big armchair with his feet up?

I let out a startled gasp. He's watching TV, I realized.

He's sitting there calmly, watching TV?

Why isn't he doing anything?

19

aybe Mr. Fleshman is waiting for reports from his agents, I told myself. I knew he had to have a plan. When I talked to him, he didn't seem worried at all.

I'll do as he instructed me, I decided. I won't go over to his house. I'll stay in my own house. I'll wait for him to announce that it's safe.

But I had to warn Mom and Dad. And I had to show them that I was telling the truth, that I wasn't making up wild stories.

I don't care how late they come home, I told myself. I'll wait up for them. And I'll force them to listen to me.

The day dragged on, the slowest, most frightening day of my life. Even with Mr. Fleshman next door, I felt so alone. So helpless.

I made myself a peanut butter sandwich for dinner. I was still hungry, so I had a bowl of cereal. And then a bag of potato chips.

I thought about poor Billie. I hoped she was okay.

Every time a car came down the street, I hurried to the front window to see if it was Mom and Dad.

The hours dragged by. I started to yawn. I felt really sleepy.

I paced back and forth, forcing myself to stay alert. I had to stay awake. I had to warn Mom and Dad about the alien invasion.

Feeling sleepier and sleepier, I turned on the TV. The eleven o'clock news had just started.

"We're expecting warmer weather in the Los Angeles area," a man was saying. "A warm front is t-t-t moving in from the San Fernando Valley, and it will bring a few showers first."

"Even the weatherman!" I moaned "Even the weatherman has been possessed by aliens!"

I forced myself to watch the whole newscast. To my horror, they never mentioned the alien landing, never mentioned the creatures that were spreading everywhere.

The sports news came on. As the sports reporter talked, green bubbles popped out of his ears. He quickly covered them up with a set of headphones.

They've all been invaded, I realized with a shudder. And they're keeping it quiet.

For how long?

Until every single person has been possessed?

A car rolled past. I ran to the window. Not Mom and Dad.

I felt so sleepy, I could barely keep my eyes open. All the tension, all the fear — it had caught up with me. I felt so weary.

I'll climb into bed and rest, I decided. I won't get undressed or anything. I'll just close my eyes for a few minutes.

When Mom and Dad get home, I'll wake up and tell them everything. . . .

"Huh?"

I woke up with a start. Bright sunlight poured into my bedroom, slanting across my bed.

I sat straight up, rubbing my eyes, confused.

I was in my jeans and T-shirt. My shoes felt as if they weighed a hundred pounds each.

I groaned.

I'd fallen asleep — and slept right through until morning.

Did Mom and Dad look in on me? Why didn't they wake me?

Were they in their room? Were they still home?

I squinted at my clock radio. Nearly ten o'clock.

How could I have slept so late? I had to talk to them! I *had* to!

I jumped up and ran out of my room. Down the stairs. "Mom? Dad?" I cried, my voice still hoarse from sleep.

"Mom? Dad? Are you home?"

I checked the kitchen. No one there.

I ran down the hall to their bedroom.

"Is anybody home?"

I pulled open the door to their bedroom — and gasped.

20

No one there.

Did I miss them? I wondered. Or did they stay at the hospital with Billie all night?

A scribbled note pinned to the refrigerator door answered my question.

Jack — We left early this morning. We hope to bring Billie home early. She's doing fine. Please get yourself to school. We'll see you later.

Love, Mom and Dad

I'll sit here and wait for them, I decided. No way I can go to school. No way I'm leaving the house.

I poured myself a glass of orange juice. Then I turned on the radio.

I flipped from station to station. Everyone I heard was clicking and going t-t-t.

No one mentioned the alien invasion.

The aliens are taking over everyone, I realized.

My throat tightened in fear. I couldn't even swallow the orange juice.

Finally, I heard a car pull up the driveway.

"Mom! Dad!" I threw open the door and went tearing up to the car.

To my surprise, I saw only Mom and Billie.

Mom climbed out and helped Billie from the passenger seat. Billie looked a little pale, a little tired. But other than that, she seemed okay.

"Mom — where's Dad?" I cried.

She brushed back her hair and uttered a weary sigh. "He had to go straight to work. Some kind of emergency."

"I *know* there's an emergency!" I cried. "Mom — I have to talk to you!" I tugged hard on her arm.

"Let me get Billie into the house first," she replied impatiently. "Are you okay? You didn't go to school?"

"No. I couldn't —" I started.

"You wanted to see your sister, huh?" Mom said. "Well, as you can see, she's going to be fine. Her throat is a little sore right now. But in a few days . . ."

"It hurts," Billie whispered, holding her throat.

"Glad you're okay," I muttered.

"I had *four* tonsils taken out," Billie whispered. "No. I had *six*!"

"Billie, don't try to talk," Mom scolded. "And stop making up wild stories."

I shook my head. Taking out her tonsils hadn't changed Billie a bit.

Mom led Billie to the back door. I hurried after them. "Mom, you've got to listen to me!" I cried. "These ugly green space creatures have landed on Earth and —"

Mom wheeled around angrily. "Jack, let's get Billie up to her room — okay?"

She pulled open the door for Billie. But Billie stopped and whispered in my ear, "I saw a space creature in the hospital. But mine was *blue*!"

"Shut up!" I screamed. "This is serious!"

"Jack, your poor sister just had an operation, and you're yelling at her?" Mom cried. "I'm ashamed of you."

Billie grinned at me. "Really. It was bright blue," she whispered. "I think it followed me home."

I stepped back. I was not in the mood to hear her dumb stories.

I let them go into the house. I waited outside, pacing back and forth nervously, kicking clumps of grass.

Finally, Mom came back out, yawning and stretching. "I didn't get much sleep last night." She sighed. "Your father and I got home very late. We looked in on you. Why were you sleeping with your clothes on, Jack?"

"Because I was waiting to talk to you!" I cried.

Mom yawned. "Go ahead. Talk." She raised her hand. "But just one thing. No more talk about space creatures and invasions. I couldn't take any more of that this morning. I'm just too tired."

I opened my mouth to start — but I stopped myself. I knew Mom wouldn't listen. I knew she wouldn't believe me.

I had to get to Dad. Maybe I stood a chance with Dad.

Dad works in the deputy mayor's office. He can talk to the deputy mayor. Maybe to the mayor. It may not be too late.

Maybe they are already dealing with the invasion. Maybe that's the emergency that forced Dad to hurry to work.

Maybe Mr. Fleshman has been in touch with the mayor's office. Maybe they're already working together to fight the aliens.

"Why didn't you go to school?" Mom asked. "Just because of Billie?"

"Uh . . . yeah," I muttered, thinking hard about getting to Dad's office downtown.

"It isn't too late to go," Mom said. "I'll write Mrs. Hoff a note."

"Okay," I said.

So I pretended to go to school.

Instead, I kept walking until I got to the bus

stop. I waited there for what seemed like days! Buses don't run that regularly in L.A.

I had to transfer twice. At one bus stop, six or seven people were all hugging each other. Behind them, a shop door stood open. I could see two people hugging in the shop doorway. Four more people were hugging on the next corner.

"Hurry! Please hurry!" I silently urged the bus driver. "I may be too late!"

The bus rumbled through the intersection. Across the street, I saw a big green creature slip into a man's back. The man's arms shot up. His mouth opened in shock. The creature vanished completely inside him.

"Did you see that?" I cried to the woman in front of me.

She muttered, "No."

No one on the bus seemed to see anything weird. No one said a word.

Have they all been invaded? I wondered.

The ride seemed to take hours. The deputy mayor's office is in one of those tall granite buildings downtown. I jumped off the bus. Tore across the street. Jumped into an open elevator and took it to the twelfth floor.

A receptionist sat behind a big desk, talking rapidly into a headphone telephone. She paused when I stepped up to the desk. "Do you have an appointment?"

103

"I have to see my dad!" I cried breathlessly. "I'm Jack Archer."

"You'll have to wait," she replied. "I think he's in with Deputy Mayor Rawls."

I couldn't wait. I lurched past her desk, into the long hall of offices.

"Hey, wait —" she shouted after me.

I bolted past two women in dark business suits, carrying identical briefcases. Past my dad's office.

The corner office was open. I saw my dad standing in the doorway, arms crossed in front of him, talking to a man behind a big desk.

"Dad!" I gasped. "Dad —!"

He turned, startled. "Jack? How did you get here?"

I burst into the office, panting, struggling to catch my breath. "Dad —?"

Dad motioned to Deputy Mayor Rawls. "You remember my son, Jack, don't you?"

Mr. Rawls nodded, smiling.

He is a big man, almost as wide as he is tall. He has bushy black hair, slicked straight back, and flashing green eyes. He wore a light blue suit. His tie dangled loosely around his open shirt collar.

"Dad — the aliens have landed!" I choked out.

Dad turned to Mr. Rawls. "Jack is very afraid of the invaders," he told him.

Mr. Rawls's smile faded quickly. He turned his big body toward me. "No need to be afraid, son," he said. "It doesn't t-t-t hurt a bit."

I gasped.

The deputy mayor turned to Dad. "Give your t-t son a nice hug, Frank."

Dad put a hand on my shoulder. He started to spin me toward him. "It'll only take a t-t-t second, Jack," Dad said softly. "Then you'll be like us."

21

"**D**ad . . . you *too!*" I shrieked.

Dad nodded grimly. Wet green bubbles slid from his ears.

"Hug him," the deputy mayor ordered. "Hug him, Frank — *now!*"

"I don't believe it." I sighed. I suddenly felt so weak and exhausted.

"It won't t-t hurt," Dad assured me again. He wrapped me in a hug.

My dad. My own dad . . .

Stunned beyond belief, I just stood there.

Defeated.

His arms tightened around my shoulders.

His fist pressed against the middle of my back.

I don't care, I thought.

It's my dad. My own dad. It's over. All over.

I can't fight him. I can't fight everyone.

I'm just one kid. I can't fight a whole city of space aliens.

I slumped weakly against my dad. I shut my eyes.

He hugged me tighter.

I heard the long nails shoot out from his fingers.

And then I felt a sharp stab of cold in the center of my back.

Like ten icicles burrowing into my skin.

The cold spreading . . . spreading . . .

22

It's over, I thought. The space creature — it's pouring into me.

Invading me.

The sharp cold tingled my skin.

My hands shot out.

My right hand hit something.

I opened my eyes in time to see the water bottle topple over.

My hand had knocked over the water bottle on Mr. Rawls's desk.

He and Dad both let out startled shrieks as water splashed over the desktop. Onto the carpet.

Mr. Rawls stared in openmouthed horror at the puddling water.

Dad jumped back.

As he let go of me, the sharp, cold feeling slid away. It vanished instantly.

I was alert now, my heart pumping.

Why did the spilled water make them jump like that? I wondered.

I didn't take time to think about it. I was free! And I was still me.

"Get him!" the deputy mayor cried. His big stomach bounced as he made a grab for me with both hands.

"Jack — t-t *stop*!" Dad called.

But I was too fast for them. I lowered my head like a football fullback and flew out of his office.

"Hey —" the receptionist called out as I bolted past her to the row of elevators. I slammed my hand on the elevator button. Then I saw a stairway at the back of the room.

"Don't let him get away, Frank!" I heard Mr. Rawls cry as they both hurtled after me. "He's just about the last one left!"

I dove for the stairs. Grabbed the metal railing as I started to fall. Then I plunged down, taking the stairs two at a time.

Footsteps thundered heavily above me.

Down one flight. I turned. Then down the next flight.

Twelve flights to the street. Could I get down them before they caught up with me? Would they be waiting for me when I reached the street?

If I did get away, where should I go? I didn't have a plan. I only knew I had to get away from them.

I was gasping for breath by the time I hit the first floor. I burst out of the stairwell and started to the exit.

"Stop right there!" a voice boomed.

Two black-uniformed security guards came running after me.

The elevator doors slid open. Dad and Mr. Rawls jumped out. "Don't let him get away!" Mr. Rawls bellowed.

I dove for the exit and shot out to the street. Blinking in the bright sunlight. Looking right, then left. Which way should I run?

The security guards came running out after me. "Freeze!" one of them ordered. The other guard was speaking rapidly into a cell phone, probably calling for other guards.

I took off, into a crowd of people. "Jack — wait! Jack!" I heard Dad calling.

Two women were hugging on the corner. I ran right into them, nearly knocking them over. "T-t-t — hey!" one of them cried out.

I shot across the street without stopping to check for traffic. Horns honked. Tires squealed.

Panting hard, I made it to the other side and glanced back. I saw *four* black-uniformed guards chasing after me now, followed by Dad and Mr. Rawls, all trotting hard, followed by two grim-faced police officers.

I let out a cry. Turned to run. Saw a city bus start to pull away from the curb.

"Please —!" I leaped to the door. Pounded my fist frantically on the glass. "Please —!"

The guards came running across the street. "Stop, kid!" one of them cried.

I pounded on the bus door. "Please —!"

Two guards grabbed for me.

The bus door slid open.

Hands grabbed my shoulders.

I jerked hard. Leaped onto the bottom step. The bus pulled away. I lurched past the driver, into a front seat.

"Fare, please," the driver called. "T-t-t pay the fare."

Struggling to catch my breath, I watched the guards, the police officers, my dad, and Mr. Rawls — all staring furiously at me from the side-walk as the bus rumbled away.

Half an hour later, I ran up the driveway to my house. I didn't see any cars in the driveway. I peeked into the windows before I went in. I had to make sure no one had followed me.

No. No one. Not yet.

Maybe they got caught in the L.A. traffic or something. But I knew they'd be here soon.

He's just about the last one left! Mr. Rawls's words repeated in my ears.

I was one of the last ones to be invaded. They wouldn't stop until they had me too.

I ran into the house. I knew I wasn't safe there.

My plan was to warn Mom and Billie. And then get over to Mr. Fleshman's house as fast as I could.

"Mom! Mom — where are you?"

"Jack? I'm up here in Billie's room," she called down.

"Well, just stay up there!" I shouted. "Stay up there where it's safe. Can you lock Billie's door?"

"Huh? Jack? What are you saying?" Mom called down.

"Just stay up there!" I cried. "I'm going to get Mr. Fleshman. He'll do something. He'll protect us."

I started to pull open the front door — but stopped when I saw the cars pull up.

At least a dozen cars. And fire trucks. And police patrol cars, their red lights flashing.

I saw Dad leap out of the first car. Then two police officers came running up the lawn, hands on their holsters.

I slammed the door shut.

My breath caught in my throat. My knees trembled, then started to collapse.

"No —!" I cried out. "I'm *not* giving up!"

I forced myself to move. I ran to the back of the house. I started to open the kitchen door.

Three black-uniformed guards turned the corner of the house and came running across the backyard.

Trapped!

I've got to get out of this house. I've got to get to Mr. Fleshman, I told myself.

But — how?

How?

I heard shouting voices outside.

Fists pounded on the door.

I peeked out through the window and saw the backyard filling with people. Neighbors came running out of their houses.

The security guards and police officers and firefighters and the mailman and several kids — they were piling into the yard, forming a circle around my house.

And as they surrounded the house, they began a low, steady chant: "A hug . . . a hug . . . a hug . . . a hug . . ."

I held my hands over my ears. But I couldn't drown out the chanting voices.

Where is Mr. Fleshman? I asked myself.

He *must* see this crowd. Why isn't he doing his job? What is he waiting for?

I turned shakily and forced myself to the basement stairs. Gripping the railing tightly, I made my way to the basement.

I stopped at the bottom of the stairs. The chanting voices seeped through the little basement windows: "A hug ... a hug ... a hug ..."

I ran through the basement — and spotted my Super Soaker water rifle on the shelf against the far wall. I stopped and stared at it — and Henry and Derek flashed into my mind. They were the best swimmers in school. But on the day of the swim team tryouts, they made excuses. They refused to get in the pool. They looked frightened.

Frightened of the water.

They had been invaded by the space alien. And suddenly, they were afraid to get wet.

And what about my dad and the deputy mayor? When I'd knocked over that bottle of water, they'd nearly jumped out of their skins.

Were they just startled?

Or were they also terrified of getting wet?

Maybe water *hurts* them, I thought. Maybe water *kills* the space aliens.

I have to give it a try, I told myself. I snatched the water rifle off the shelf and raced to the sink in the laundry room. I'll blast everyone out of my way. Maybe I can get to Mr. Fleshman's house.

My hands were trembling so hard, I could barely fill it.

Water splashed all over the basement floor. But

I filled the big water tank. And then I pumped the rifle, pumped it and pumped it until it was ready.

"This has to work," I muttered to myself. "This has to help me get next door." I forced myself up the stairs. I made my way to the front door. My whole body was trembling. The Super Soaker rifle felt heavier and heavier in my hands.

"A hug . . . a hug . . . a hug . . ."

I could hear the eerie, steady chant.

I peeked out. The possessed people had formed a ring around the house. I recognized Henry and Derek in the front of the crowd. Dad stood nearby, chanting along with the others.

"Here goes," I told myself.

I took a deep breath.

I raised the heavy water rifle onto my shoulder.

I pulled open the front door and stepped outside.

The chant stopped instantly. Some people cried out in surprise. Others cheered. Then the circle of people moved in on me quickly.

As they surged forward, they stretched out their arms. And began to chant again. "A hug . . . give him a hug . . . a hug . . . give him a hug . . ."

Closer. Closer.

Reaching out. Reaching for me . . .

"I'm sorry!" I shouted. "But I have no choice!"

I lowered the Super Soaker from my shoulder. Pulled the trigger in. And shot a hard stream of water into the crowd.

The stream of water hit a man in the chest. He coiled back in surprise.

I heard startled cries.

I swerved the rifle quickly, trying to spray everyone in my way. I sprayed two kids. They tossed up their arms and dropped back.

The powerful stream splashed over the front of a police officer's dark shirt. He glared at me and didn't budge.

I heard laughter now.

"A squirt gun!" someone jeered. "He thinks a stupid squirt gun will stop us!"

More laughter.

The crowd moved in. Arms outstretched. Hands reaching for me.

"A hug . . . give him a hug . . ."

I lowered the Super Soaker rifle. Water dribbled onto my shoes.

Henry and Derek were laughing. "Did you think that would t-t stop us?" Derek cried.

"But — but at school —" I stammered. "You wouldn't swim —!"

They laughed again. "We just didn't feel like it," Henry said. He laughed. "Water doesn't hurt us a bit."

He stepped up to me, so much bigger than me, and stronger. "Hug time, Jack," he murmured.

"No —!" I dropped the plastic rifle. I took another step back.

I gasped when I saw Mom. She had come outside. She was standing next to Dad. They had their arms around each other. And they were both chanting, "A hug . . . a hug . . . give him a hug," clapping their hands in rhythm to the chant.

"Nooooo —!" A horrified cry escaped my throat.

I staggered back, searching for a hole in the circle of people. Some way to escape.

I spun all the way around.

No way. No way.

Hands reached for me. The chanting crowd lumbered closer.

And then I spotted Mr. Fleshman.

Finally!

He stood behind the circle of people at the side of the garage. He was dressed in black, as usual.

His silvery hair caught the sunlight, making it appear as if his whole head were glowing.

"Mr. Fleshman —!" I called, shouting over the rumbling chant. "What is happening?"

He stepped away from the garage. Took a few steps toward me, hands on his waist.

"You promised!" I cried. "You promised the space creatures would all be gone in a day or two!"

He pushed through the crowd. He strode up to me, his silver eyes locked on mine.

"We *will* be gone, Jack," he said. "We'll be gone as soon as we take care of you."

I gasped. My heart jumped.

"You mean — you're *one* of them?" I cried.

"Jack," he replied. "I'm their leader."

Mr. Fleshman raised a hand high above his head. The chanting stopped. The crowd grew silent.

He stood over me, silver eyes gleaming. "I'm their leader," he explained, speaking in that hoarse, whispery voice. "I'm their power source. All of their energy comes from me."

"But — but —" I sputtered weakly.

I turned away. Those strange eyes, burning into me, were too frightening now.

"I came here first, to set up a base," Mr. Fleshman continued. "To make sure Earth was ready for us. I built all the special effects in my house to make people think I had a job."

A strange smile spread over his tanned face. "Do you know my *best* special effect? It's this human body."

"Huh?" I gasped.

Still grinning, Mr. Fleshman reached both hands up to his face.

He tugged hard.

The skin began to slide.

He pulled with both hands, pulling at his throat, then his chest.

His face, his skin, his clothing — he tugged it all off. It made a sick, wet *SLLLLLUUUUPPPP* as it slid away.

Then he bundled it up and tossed it in a heap on the ground.

I gaped at him in horror. He didn't look like the other aliens. He looked like an enormous *brain*! His body pulsed and throbbed, pink and wet.

Electrical sparks shot off all around him. He crackled as he moved, as if surrounded by electrical current.

A bright red hole near the top of the throbbing pink body opened and closed. His mouth. "I am the power source!" Mr. Fleshman declared.

The possessed crowd cheered their leader.

"I waited so long for my friends to arrive, Jack." The hole opened and closed, allowing the words to escape from deep inside the pulsing, brainlike mound. "Waited for them to come get their fresh bodies. Now we all have human bodies, bodies that will work well on our planet."

"Oh, no," I moaned. "You mean —"

The pulsing mound bobbed excitedly. "Yes, it's

121

time to go. Time to go back to our planet with our new bodies. I promised you we'd be gone — didn't I?"

"Yes, but —" I swallowed hard.

"There's just one problem," Mr. Fleshman said, leaning over me. "You're the last holdout, Jack," he growled. "The last holdout in town. We need your body, Jack. We can't leave you behind."

He rose up in front of me. Sparks flew off his body.

"A hug — now," he declared.

"Please —" I begged. "Please don't."

"We need every body," the red mouth at the top of the throbbing brain pronounced.

"No —!" I begged. I turned to Mom and Dad. They stood in the crowd, their arms still around each other.

"It won't hurt, Jack," Dad called. "It only t-t-t takes a second."

Mr. Fleshman's pink, wet flesh began to wrap around me.

I heard the buzz of electricity. Felt my skin tingle where he touched me.

"A hug, Jack," Mr. Fleshman rasped. "A hug."

I let out a long sigh. My whole body slumped as the creature wrapped me up.

I can't fight it, I realized.

I can't fight them all. There's just no point.

Even my parents are under his power.

"Okay," I whispered. "Okay."

"Okay." I gave up. I let my body go slack.

Mr. Fleshman's crackling body wrapped me in a warm, sticky hug. Bright yellow sparks flew all around. He smelled smoky, as if he were on fire. As if the electrical current were burning the soft pink flesh.

I'm gone now, I thought. I'm gone.

The heavy flesh closed tightly around me. Surrounded me. Cut off my air.

A powerful electric shock made me shudder.

The shock woke me up.

I had an idea. A crazy, desperate idea.

I raised my hands. Grabbed at the alien's brain-like mass.

I tensed every muscle. Tensed them so hard, they hurt.

I gritted my teeth. Set my jaw. Tightened my arms, my legs.

And burst into the creature's back!

I slid inside Mr. Fleshman. Into a deep darkness. Into pulsing heat. Into a strong, steady, throbbing current.

Inside. Inside. Inside.

I heard him cry out in shock.

Inside him — in the dark, wet, throbbing heat — I felt him squirm and struggle.

I had turned everything around. He tried to invade me — but I invaded him first. Pushed myself into the pulsing current, into the energy, into his *mind*!

From inside, I heard the roar of protest rumble up from his big belly. Heard the roar explode from his gaping mouth.

And then I felt the big body tremble. Tremble so hard, it fell in on itself.

I sank with it, sank to the ground.

I felt all of the creature's muscles sag. Felt his massive body collapse.

Mr. Fleshman plunged facedown. I plunged with him.

Down . . . down . . . so far to fall, and so heavy.

I thudded hard. Bounced twice.

He didn't move. *We* didn't move.

I forced myself up. Using every muscle, every ounce of strength, I forced myself up — and out.

Out of the meaty, hot alien body.

I grabbed the side of the house. Gasping for air. Dripping with sweat. I spun around. And saw Mr. Fleshman — the leader, the power source — lying dead at my feet.

I invaded him. *And it killed him.*

Gasping, choking, my body still trembling, still tingling from the heat inside the alien's body, I raised my eyes to the crowd.

And saw them coming for me.

Marching . . . marching heavily, with dead eyes, on dead legs, marching, marching . . .

"Ohhh . . ." With a moan of horror, I sank back against the wall of the house.

The possessed people thudded toward me, trudging heavily. I saw Marsha and Maddy, their eyes dead, their jaws slack, arms outstretched.

Mom and Dad . . . Henry and Derek . . . police officers . . . neighbors . . . marching . . . marching.

And then they all stopped. And collapsed to their knees. All of them. All at once.

And the green creatures slid out. The big green aliens slid onto the grass. Sprawled there. And didn't move.

"The energy source," I muttered, watching in amazement. "Mr. Fleshman was the energy source. I killed it. I killed the energy source."

One by one, the humans all climbed up from

their knees. They stretched their arms. They took deep breaths. They stepped away from the dead aliens. They began to smile, to laugh.

And then they seemed to see me for the first time.

"You saved us!" a woman cried.

"You defeated them, Jack!"

"You did it!"

"You saved us all!"

"Jack, you're a hero!" Maddy declared.

The backyard rang out with cheers and happy cries.

Mom and Dad rushed forward and hugged me. This time, I didn't mind being hugged!

People began to sing, to dance! Everyone was so happy to be free, to be safe. What a scene of celebration!

I watched happily for a moment. And then a name escaped my throat. "Billie!"

My sister. Where was she?

I realized Billie had been up in her room the whole time.

Was she okay?

I spun away from the gleeful, cheering crowd and dove into the house. "Billie? Billie?" I called her name as I ran up the stairs to her room.

"Billie?"

"I'm still here." She raised her head from the pillow and pulled herself up on her elbows as I burst into her room.

"Are you okay?" I cried.

"I saw you," she said, still whispering because of her throat. "I saw you from the window, Jack. You were great!"

"Thanks," I said. I stared hard at her. Billie had never said anything that nice about me before! "Are you okay? I was worried —"

"You defeated the green creatures," Billie whispered. She struggled up to a sitting position. "But what about my *blue* creature?"

"Huh?" I narrowed my eyes at her.

"I told you — I found a space creature too!" she declared in her hoarse whisper. "Mine is blue — and it's bigger than yours!"

"Billie, please!" I wailed. "Let's stop competing, okay? No more wild stories. Okay?"

I heard a loud rumble. Billie's closet door crashed open. The wood splintered.

An enormous blue monster staggered out.

"See?" Billie declared. "He wants a hug, Jack. Give him a hug."

About R.L. Stine

R.L. Stine is the most popular author in America. He is the creator of the *Goosebumps*, *Give Yourself Goosebumps*, *Fear Street*, and *Ghosts of Fear Street* series, among other popular books. He has written nearly 200 scary novels for kids. Bob lives in New York City with his wife, Jane, teenage son, Matt, and dog, Nadine.

Welcome to the new millennium of fear

Check out this
chilling preview of
what's next from
R.L. STINE

I Am Your
Evil Twin

e know you did it, Monty,"
Mrs. Williams said. "An-
other student saw you. Unless you can tell us why
Ashley would lie about something like that."

"I don't know!" I cried. "But I know I didn't
trash the art room. And I've never been to your
office before, Mrs. Williams. I've never even met
you before!"

Mrs. Williams studied my face as if she couldn't
believe what she was hearing.

"I know it's hard, Monty," she said quietly. "I
know it's not easy adjusting to a new school and a
new home."

I bit my lip. I wanted to scream. No matter
what I said, she'd never believe me.

"But this behavior is unacceptable," she went
on. "And lying about it only makes things worse."

"I'm telling the truth!" I insisted.

Mrs. Williams shook her head. "I'm willing to give you one more chance. But this lying must stop. Go back to the art room and clean up that mess. And I don't want to see you in my office again."

I trudged back to the art room with slumping shoulders.

This is a nightmare! I thought. What is happening to me?

I found cleaning supplies in a cupboard and got to work. This is going to take hours, I realized. It's so unfair!

I gathered up the trash on the floor and threw it away. With a sigh, I started scrubbing the paint off one of the walls.

Then, out of the corner of my eye, I caught a sudden movement in the window. I glanced to my right.

My own face stared in at me — wiry red hair, big nose, and all.

My heart stood still for a moment.

Then I realized I was simply seeing my reflection in the window glass.

Get a grip, Monty! I told myself. I turned away and started scrubbing again.

Another flash of movement at the window. I glanced around sharply. Was there someone out there?

Again, I found myself staring at my reflection.

It seemed awfully sharp and clear. Maybe because the day was so dark, I thought. I frowned.

My reflection frowned.

Weird. I noticed something squinty about my eyes. A sly gleam. Do I really look like that? I wondered.

I stuck out my tongue.

My reflection stuck out its tongue.

I raised my left hand and waggled my fingers.

My reflection didn't move.

PREPARE TO BE SCARED!

Goosebumps®
SERIES 2000
R.L. STINE

▲■SCHOLASTIC   ✳ PARACHUTE